W9-AVR-135

The **JAWS**fest Murders

This book is dedicated to:

June Houston (Grandma)
Lynne McLean (Aunt Lynnie)
I wish you both could have read this.
&
Dalores Haskins (Nana)
Always, always, my biggest supporter.

This book is also dedicated to my fellow JAWS 'FINatics'. While the events and characters in The JAWSfest Murders are completely fictional, I have paid homage to some of you by using your home states and countries. You know who you are. Thank you for continuing to share JAWS with me.

The **JAWS**fest Murders

A Martha's Vineyard Mystery

By

Crispin Nathaniel Haskins

1

When he fell, the man smashed his head against a tree stump wedging a piece of bark into his eye. It was too dark to see the stump coming so he had done nothing to break his fall. The pain was sharp, almost unbearable but he stumbled back onto his feet and tried to keep going. The woods were dark, very dark. In the horror movies of his youth, there always seemed to be this incredible moonlight to guide people's paths through the woods but in real life, there was nothing but oily blackness. His lungs were burning and for a brief moment he regretted giving up his gym membership. It seemed like a ridiculous thing to think about given his current situation but he decided he would rejoin if he got out of these woods alive. He stopped running for just a second to feel his eye and catch his breath. The eye was intact but there was a warm, stickiness pumping out of a three-inch gash below his brow. He knew he was bleeding pretty badly.

The dark, the blood, and the swelling had rendered that eye useless. There wasn't much to see but having the use of two eyes would definitely have been a plus. There was a snapping noise behind him on his left. He reached out and groped for cover. Lowering his breath as much as he could, he felt for the stump. If he snuggled up to it tightly, he thought, he and the stump might just pass as one. His breathing sounded like trumpets over the marching band of his heartbeat. It all sounded so loud to him; he couldn't believe that he hadn't been caught and killed by now. This was not the Martha's Vineyard he knew. The footsteps came closer. They were slow and methodical. His hunter was no more than forty feet directly in front of him. His outline was barely discernable in the blackness but his movement gave him away. It seemed like he had been hunting his prey by listening to his footsteps but now that they had stopped, the hunter was confused and cautious. He kept moving, slowly but with purpose. He hardly made a sound.

The man beside the tree stump watched almost numb as his hunter crept past him. The plan seemed to have worked. He watched and listened as intently as he could before standing up. It had gone quiet. His legs had cramped up while he had huddled against the stump and it was hard to move. His hamstrings screamed as he straightened and he got a Charlie-horse in one of his calves. Running through the woods had made him cold and wet. He stood and started in the opposite direction of the hunter. There needed to be as much distance between the two of them as possible. He needed to make it to the police station in Edgartown but fast. He wasn't even sure where he was or in which direction he was headed. He had been running in the woods for what seemed an eternity and it was impossible to tell whether he had moved in a straight line or not. He did know that he had to get out of the woods. If he got out of the woods, he'd be safe.

He couldn't help but scream out but he wasn't sure if he was screaming due to the sound of the gunshot or because of the bullet tearing off the top half of his ear. His face burned, his ear burned. He was crying now. His wails were more than enough to give away his exact location no matter how dark it was or how fast he ran. He couldn't help himself. His head was spinning and he thought he was going to be sick. The second shot sounded through the forest and he felt like he had been kicked to the ground by a heavy boot. He landed face first in the muck. The wind knocked out of him, he pleaded for air but found very little. He realised that he had been shot in the back. He would not live through this; he knew that now. His mouth was filling with a thick metallic taste. He had stopped wailing and was gurgling up blood instead. He tried to get to his feet but he barely managed to roll over. Up through the trees, he saw the moon come out from behind the cloud cover. He couldn't feel his hands or feet. The forest lit up just like in the movies. He felt the warmth of his bladder let go in his jeans. Trees were a haunting blue in the moonlight, so were

9

the ferns, moss, and grass- he saw the stump that he had hit. The light faded again. There was something peaceful about a forest at night. It was beautiful. A calm. The man was dead.

2

It was impossible for Charles to stop smiling as he watched the island get closer on the horizon. He hadn't been on Martha's Vineyard for decades and he was *so* excited about being back; he could hardly stand still in his spot on the upper-deck of the ferry. Everything was how he remembered it or at least, how he had imagined that he remembered it. How much of his thoughts were actual memories was impossible to tell. He had spent years reading about the island. Not to mention the hours that he had spent watching videos about Edgartown, Chilmark, Vineyard Haven, Oak Bluffs, Aquinnah, and Chappaquiddick all posted on YouTube. His own memories from childhood vacations were muddled in there somewhere too. Trips with his Mom and Dad were mixed with fantasies of returning. As a child, he had camped in Edgartown, swam on South Beach, shopped through Oak Bluffs, rode the Flying Horse Carousel, and swam in the

Inkwell. Then of course there were the pop culture references that he devoured at every opportunity. Philip R. Craig had written wonderful Martha's Vineyard Mysteries that had afforded Charles vacations on his beloved island when he could not afford them any other way. His novels spoke so lovingly and so clearly of the Vineyard that you could smell the tide going out in the evening and taste the salt on your lips from a swim. Cynthia Riggs wrote Martha's Vineyard mysteries as well and her central characters jumped off of the page with richness equal to those of Mr Craig. In Charles' mind, their two worlds existed simultaneously creating a complete picture. Memories, videos, books, articles, movies, they all blended into a magical, delicious treat that Charles had permanently baked in his head. Then, there was JAWS. JAWS had been filmed on Martha's Vineyard. Not only was it Charles' favourite movie, it was Charles' favourite subject- period. For whatever reason, when it came out in the summer of 1975, JAWS hit Charles like a tonne of bricks. He figured that it was because at the time, there was no other way to see sharks. Not like there was today anyway. Sure, sharks were fascinating animals but they would probably have about as much coverage on The Discovery Channel as the Polar Bear if it weren't for JAWS. JAWS came first. In fact, it was because of JAWS that all of those other movies, TV specials, and tourist attractions existed and it had all started here on Martha's Vineyard. Charles had been almost hypnotized watching Chief & Mrs Brody, Mayor Vaughn, Hooper, and Quint, all of his childhood heroes, running around 'Amity Island' and heading to sea to fight an enormous great white shark. When he and his Dad went to the Vineyard for the first time together, it drove the magic of the island and the movie home in his young head. Life wasn't imitating art; life had become art. At the age of six, it was hard to wrap his mind around the fact that he was in Amity – the fictitious island of his favourite movie. It was hard to separate the movie when he watched it from his favourite vacation with his Dad. The two were identical. The Vineyard certainly didn't change. Amity was Martha's Vineyard and vice versa. Weather-greyed, cedar shingle houses, fishing boats, rolling waves on South Beach, calm family swimming on State Beach, the perfectly white whaling village of Edgartown and the red brick of the Gay Head lighthouse, they were all there on the big screen. Charles even played the old video game 'Killer Shark' which featured prominently in the movie just to drive the illusion home further. Martha's Vineyard caught a lot of people in its magic. It was idyllic- that was undeniable. But with Charles, it caught him early and he had never been able to get out of its net. Of course, he had never really tried either.

Charles watched Oak Bluffs get closer as the ferry turned to begin docking. Seagulls that followed the ferry from Woods Hole for the French fries tossed by its generous passengers now fled in search of bigger treats on the Vineyard. It was early, not even lunch yet but the sun was high and bright. The clouds, if you could call them that, were more whiffs of steam from a distant and invisible locomotive. It was unseasonably hot. A small line up (small by summer standards but it was early on a Wednesday) of cars and trucks waited to get off the island and the large crowd waiting to disembark had already started to form their line without waiting for instruction from the crew. There were no Vineyard virgins here. Well-seasoned 'summer dinks' were these. The boat stopped. The chains dropped. The doors opened. They had arrived.

*   *   *

Walking onto Martha's Vineyard, Charles was nervous with excitement. He was on his Vineyard. It was completely familiar and yet completely foreign. First thing to do was to get to his hotel. He was in Oak Bluffs but he was staying at The Edgartown Inn. He had friends who were staying within walking distance of the ferry terminal but he preferred the calm, elegant feel of Edgartown to the touristy bar and party scene of Oak Bluffs. At night, Edgartown made you feel like you were dining with the Kennedys while a night in Oak Bluffs could make you feel like you were watching Jersey Shore. He walked away from the boat and looked for an information booth. It really had been a while. Charles was very pleasantly directed toward the bus stop; it was in Ocean View Park just two short blocks up the street. There he found a volunteer senior citizen selling tickets and bus passes. Many of the islanders volunteered during the tourist season. A spritely woman with a big smile and a silver bob gave Charles the rundown on the buses. "It's a $2 trip to Edgartown." She stated clearly. "The island transit system charges $1 per town and that includes the town you start in. Okay, love? You can get a day pass for $7, a three day for $15, and it's $25 for the week. They take dollar bills on the bus. Do you need to buy a pass?" Charles had the correct change and told her that he would hold off on the pass for now. He got on the bus that was waiting and sat down by an open window, relieved to be able to take off his heavy knapsack.

The bus headed down Seaview Avenue with Oak Bluffs on the right hand side and the Atlantic Ocean on the left. Charles couldn't decide where to look. On the right, Ocean Park and the bandstand surrounded by beautiful, multi-coloured homes that made Oak Bluffs famous and on the left, the ocean itself in all of its majestic beauty. The beach was not busy but certainly in use and sailboats raced by in the distance occasionally breaking up the golden sparkle of the sun on the water. It was picture perfect. As they lumbered on, Seaview Avenue turned into Beach Road and they continued toward Edgartown.

Sengekontacket Pond crept up on the right hand side and then, more importantly to Charles, State Beach began to appear on his left and he grinned with excitement. This was a JAWS beach. Alex Kintner had been eaten on this beach. The man in the red rowboat had been killed on this beach. Chief Brody had run along the rock wall to drag his son, Michael, out of the water on this beach. This site was a big deal to JAWS fanatics or 'FINatics' as they had dubbed themselves. Nothing had changed. It was like driving onto a movie set. Charles got closer to the window to inhale every bit of the sea air that he could. His face hurt from smiling. Kids were jumping off the JAWS bridge as the bus rolled across. Charles loved the fact that even in tourist brochures The American Legion Memorial Bridge had become known as the 'JAWS Bridge' and that 'JAWS Bridge Jumping' had become a tradition. It was all Charles could do not to get off the bus and jump into the pond with them. First order of business had to be to check into The Edgartown Inn. Once that was settled and Charles was sure that he had a home, he could do as he pleased. He watched the kids swim to the jetty, climb out onto the rocks, and run to jump in again. There was something to be said for a vacation hot spot that was known for great white sharks and still couldn't keep tourists out of the water. The thought made Charles smile. When he saw the purple sign with gold writing that read 'Welcome to Edgartown est. 1671' he knew he was getting close.

Charles stepped off the bus and looked around. This was not a bus stop in Toronto, that's for sure! The bus stop was all but hidden behind a tiny parkette with large leafy trees and park benches. The building itself had a convenience store/visitor's centre inside and bathrooms outside to the left. The bus stop was weather-greyed, wooden shingles with white wooden posts. Charles didn't recall any of Toronto's bus stops serving ice cream but he thought that the islanders were definitely onto something there. Different line-ups on the interlocking brick of the park were all waiting for different buses but the longest line-up was the one for the number thirteen to Oak Bluffs. Charles pulled his iPhone out of his shorts and opened up the GPS. He typed in the address of The Edgartown Inn and instantly a little blue light flashed indicating Charles' position and a red light indicated his destination. He wasn't far. Turning to his right, he headed up Church Street.

Edgartown unfolded in front of him in a seemingly unending collection of white wooden houses with black shutters. The narrow streets were lined with even narrower lawns dotted with rich, green, deciduous trees. Black-eyed Susans, red and white roses, and rich pink and periwinkle blue hydrangeas, all bloomed as far as the eye could see. Charles didn't really understand how you got both pink and blue hydrangeas on the same plant; it was his understanding that the colour depended on the soil's pH balance. He would have to look that up later. He was always looking things up later.

Following the directions on his iPhone, Charles turned right at Peases Point Way and then after a very short block of perfectly manicured homes on his left and tall pine trees on his right, he turned right again at Simpson Lane. Streets, avenues, roads, and lanes were all the same thing to him but if this was any indication, lanes were very narrow. Charles kept to the left on Simpson Lane and wondered if he should be on it at all. If a car were to go by it would be a very tight squeeze indeed. It was high season on the Vineyard so he assumed that the locals would chalk it up to just another tourist who didn't know any better. There was new construction on the lane so the smell of wood chips was strong. It was a rich natural smell and it made Charles think of northern Ontario and the cottage back in Canada. It seemed ridiculous to him to be in the middle of living his long time fantasy of returning to Martha's Vineyard and be dreaming of northern Ontario at the same time. Charles had come up to a weathered grey building on his left. He recognised the sign immediately: a large red, white, and blue plaque with a stylized whale in the centre. The Edgartown Inn, it read.

3

As he walked up the half a dozen stairs leading to the front porch, Charles was greeted by an assortment of welcomes, smiles, and "Hellos". The porch was perfect. It spanned the entire front of the inn and was about ten feet deep on the north end and five feet deep on the south. A sturdy roof held up by freshly painted white columns and a surrounding four-foot wall gave it full coverage. The green outdoor/indoor carpet was clean and a bit worn but probably had one more season in it. Guests were lounging on white wicker furniture. The green and white striped, over-stuffed cushions looked extremely comfortable. Some people were reading while others just watched the people go by on North Water Street. Charles decided right then and there that this was where he would have his morning coffee. The spring on the screen door groaned as Charles opened it and stepped inside.

The front hall of The Edgartown Inn was decorated in rich colours and mariner trinkets. A stairway climbed the right wall of the foyer and the left wall directed you down the hallway to the heart of the building. Charles walked the burgundy carpet past the library (he recognised it from their website) and to the front desk- such that it was. Charles had worked in the hotel industry and to him 'front desk' implied the epicentre of the hotel's activity. The front desk was a large hub where bellmen, housekeepers, and guests alike discussed the needs of the day, going and coming at a hectic pace. It was hard to imagine *this* front desk being the epicentre of anything and he would *certainly* not describe it as a large hub. The heart of The Edgartown Inn was where the main hallway opened up into a space of about eight by ten feet. All of the walls were papered in green wallpaper that had a nautical motif but they were covered with so many framed photographs and paintings that you could hardly see it. There was a beautiful grandfather clock on the west wall and an archway that led to the dining room. The south wall framed an open door where Charles could see a maid cleaning a guestroom. It must be his room, thought Charles. It was three hours before check-in and really, how many people could this place be expecting on a Wednesday? The north wall had a table and chair and on the table was a large open book where guests signed their name, address, and phone number with an attached pen. Beside the table was a half door that segregated what could only be the employee office from the rest of the house. Charles felt like he had stepped back about sixty years! No sign of a computer or any modern machinery anywhere. He had only seen a hotel office like this in the Bates Motel in Psycho. He half expected to see Norman Bates pop out of the half door. He didn't. Actually, no one did. Upon closer inspection, Charles noticed there was a sign perched on the half-door. "I'm in the garden!!" it read cheerfully.

The lights were off in the dining room but the big windows with the homemade sheer curtains let in more than enough light for Charles to see his path through a charming dining room to the back of the house. Charles pushed open another screen door. "Hello??" he called. It's hard to get loud without sounding pushy.

"I'm coming!!" He could hear her but he couldn't see her. "I'll be right there." From around the corner came a pretty, round-faced woman whom Charles could tell had been very beautiful in her youth but had now comfortably settled on attractive. Her natural hair bounced between wavy and curly and it had been highlighted and low-lighted to hide the grey. She wore a black dress that showed off her cleavage and a comfy pair of mules. Not exactly gardening wear but Charles was sure that The Edgartown Inn was the kind of place that made employees wear all different hats during a shift. She looked up at him. Her chubby face forced her eyes to squint just a little when she smiled. It was a good smile. It was the well-practiced industry smile that Charles had seen a million times. It was the genuine smile of a 'people person' and it said, "I'm going to give you the benefit of the doubt and treat you like my best friend...until you piss me off". Charles had one just like it. "Hi! I'm Edie! Are you Charles?" Edie stretched out her hand and gave Charles a firm handshake.

"Yes Ma'am. Are you the lady I spoke with on the phone?" Charles always got extremely polite when he travelled. He had no idea why- best foot forward and all that.

"I ...think so... Where are you coming in from again Charles?" Edie looked at him intently.

"Toronto...Canada." He remembered vaguely that there was at least one Toronto in the United States...Ohio, he thought.

"Yes! That was me! You called when I was in Florida back in, oh god, March, I think! I remember now." She flicked her hand in mild disgust. "Sorry, it took me a minute but that's one of the sure signs of age. I have a good memory; it's just short." She laughed at her own joke. "Would you sign the registry for me please, Charles?" She motioned toward the large book on the table. Once again Charles marvelled at its use as an actual journal of business.

"Certainly." Charles looked at all of the names above his and followed their lead. He wrote very legibly.

"Have you been to the island before?"

"Yes ma'am but not for some time now. I used to summer here as a child with my parents." He finished writing and looked at Edie. "I've been really excited about returning and hope to make it a regular thing."

"That's great. Just here to relive some memories...make new ones." She winked. "What made you decide to come now?"

"Well, this is where my story takes on a slightly geeky bent to it," he said sheepishly. "I'm here for JAWSfest."

Edie tossed her curls back and laughed. "That's great!!" she said clapping her hands in glee. "We love JAWS on this island! So many of my friends were in that movie. I saw it not too long ago! Oh, that's going to be a lot of fun. They've got quite a bit planned for you guys. The woman who has organised the whole thing is a good girlfriend of mine. She's really put a lot of hard work into it." And then, almost under her breath she said, "You know, there have been a few Great White Shark sightings around the island lately. It seems that you and your friends aren't the only ones showing up for JAWSfest!"

Charles thought how nice it was to mention JAWS and not see that polite and all too familiar glazed look that came over the faces of his family and friends when he spouted yet another fact about giant rubber sharks, Amity island, and/or Steven Spielberg. Just to be able to talk to people with a similar interest would make the trip worth it.

"Okay, Charles this is your room, right here, behind you that Alexandra is finishing up." She pointed across the hall at the room Charles had seen when he arrived and the housekeeper looked up and smiled at the mention of her name. He knew it was his room. "Now, let me just tell you your balance so we can get that out of the way..." she tapered off as she flipped through her balance books to find his bill. He couldn't believe that she did this all manually.

Charles looked at his balance and reached into his pocket to produce the cash. After he paid, Edie walked out from behind the half-door and showed Charles into his room. She pointed out the amenities, gave Charles his key, and made her exit.

Charles liked his room a lot. It smelled great. There was a queen size bed in the centre with high pillows and a spotless white bedspread. The carpet was green and there was matching wainscoting with a white chair rail. Above that, the walls were papered with a pattern of red poppies and blue cornflowers. It was very Victorian right down to the leather wingback chair and cherry wood writers' desk. The room, like the rest of the inn, was very welcoming and very clean. Charles walked through to the bathroom. It was large and white. The bathtub was a large square nestled in the corner with a curtain that pulled around two sides of the tub. At six feet and one inch and weighing over two hundred and twenty pounds, Charles was not a small man and the thought of a large square shower was very appealing. After a day of travel, he could use one. Charles opened his bag and put his clothes away in the dresser. He stripped off and showered before heading out for lunch.

As soon as Charles stepped out onto the porch, he could see the ocean. He headed straight for it. He knew that there would be plenty of restaurants on Edgartown Harbour. He crossed North Water Street and headed down Daggett Street. Daggett Street was straight downhill. About one hundred metres in front of him at the bottom of the street, he saw cars lining up and it dawned on him where he was. He was at the 'On Time III' ferry to Chappaquiddick aka the 'Amity On Time' in JAWS! Charles beamed with delight as he walked the street his hero, Chief Brody, had driven down to warn the boy scouts who were swimming for their merit badges. He wasn't going to make it to lunch right away; this had to be savoured for a minute or two. He walked down the hill to the ferry and watched. It was the middle of the season, so there were two ferries working at all times. One was docking at Chappy on the far side and one had just arrived on the Edgartown side too. In honour of JAWSfest, the 'On Time III' ferry had put up their signs from the film that said, 'Amity On Time'. That was great. Charles took out his iPhone and took a few pictures. He loved everything about this island. If this had been anywhere else, they would have built a bridge or a tunnel, years ago but on Martha's Vineyard, the island that still didn't even have a *traffic* light, this ferry was more than adequate. So for now, the Chappaquiddick ferry would continue it's 500 foot run. Charles had taken it many times as a child. He walked over and read the sign. Round trips were $4 for walk-ons, $6 if you had a bike ($8 if it was motorized), and $12 for cars. Trailers, of course, were extra depending on length. It had been running for 200 years and knowing how islanders hated change, it would continue for the next 200, Charles mused. "If it ain't broke, don't fix it" seemed to be the island motto and that was a great part of its charm. Charles really was hungry now and he headed down Dock Street in search of the world's greatest lobster roll.

He had been right. There was certainly no shortage of eateries on the waterfront. He had hit tourist central of Edgartown and every second building was a restaurant that wanted you to taste its wares. Even though it was the hub of Edgartown's tourism, it was lovely. Edgartown tourism consisted of art shops and galleries, restaurants and cafes. Greenery was well manicured and spotted with sculptures telling the tale of the harbour's past in the whaling industry- tourism at its most elegant. The streets at the harbour were narrow and riddled with pedestrians and cyclists. Drivers had a hard time of it driving downtown mid-season. There seemed to be a uniform among the people of Edgartown: button-down Oxfords, Polo shirts, khaki walking shorts, and deck shoes- no socks. Men and women all wore the same thing. It seemed to Charles that everyone was prepared in case one of the Kennedys were to jump off of a yacht and asked them to go for a champagne sail. It probably happened all the time.

There was no litter in Edgartown. There were a lot of people everywhere and even though everyone seemed to be sipping or munching on something, the streets were very clean. Charles hadn't gone far when he came across The Seafood Shanty's outdoor patio that looked over the water. That was it for him. He walked in and was directed to a table for two at the very back, as close to the water as he could be. Perfect. He ordered a pint of Stella and was left to peruse the menu. Disappointingly, the lobster roll sounded completely lack-lustre. He would know the lobster roll for him when he saw it. Surprising himself, he ordered the burger. Charles decided that he should have looked for something appetizing on the menu posted out front instead of drooling over the view but then again, they should have put some money into the food instead of cashing in on the view, which was magnificent. Charles focused there.

It was mid-day and mid-August. Sailboats and all other manner of recreational boats smoothed through the water. Charles watched their various wakes lap and roll into small waves that inevitably crashed and disappeared against the motorboats tied up in dock. There was no better place in the world. No one was in a bad mood. Shoppers walked by just below him laughing, tossing their blonde heads back on their way to their next purchase. Charles looked at his iPhone; he had six hours until he met his

JAWSfest friends at Seasons Bar in Oak Bluffs. He was really looking forward to that. He had never met any of them and yet, he felt closer to them than some of the people that he saw everyday. That was the power of Facebook.

It wasn't that long ago that Charles had been completely anti-Facebook but after being home for months with a severe concussion from a bike accident, he had caved in out of sheer boredom. For someone as social as Charles, Facebook had been the ideal escape from his dark apartment and convalescence. His friends and family all laughed at him now as he was on Facebook more than anyone else they knew. He prided himself on being told repeatedly that he "gave good Facebook". That he was certainly the most entertaining Facebook user. He loved that. He didn't want to be one of these people who just typed, "going to the fridge now" or "I'm having a terrible day! I need a hug!!" and "making dinner with the hubby!!" Charles wondered if there were really people out there who gave a shit about that sort of thing but then again, after finding out what 'Jersey Shore' was, nothing surprised him anymore. He had sat through ten minutes of that show once and had decided that, given the choice, he would rather have his eyeballs removed with a melon-baller. Charles had absolutely no interest in using Facebook to look up old acquaintances either. He figured if he still liked them, he would still know them. A couple of people had sought him out and he had accepted one or two friend requests but for the most part, he used Facebook as a creative monologue and a way to pursue his own interests just like any other part of the internet. The JAWS group had become a big part of his life.

The JAWS group consisted of about one hundred and fifty members. Charles did not remember joining. He assumed that it was recommended to him by someone on the 'JAWSmovie' website; he had been on that for years. Charles checked in on the Facebook JAWS group every other day in the beginning- posting pictures and videos, commenting on others' posts. He enjoyed it. That had led to private messages with a few of the regulars. Now, there was a core group of them that numbered in the fifties, who talked a couple of times a day. They lived in Spain, Britain, Australia, and all over North America. When Martha's Vineyard had decided to put on another JAWSfest, Charles had decided that enough was enough- he was going. He had longed to go back to the island, he loved JAWS, and he really wanted to meet his friends of some two years now!! How could he not?

Charles' hamburger and fries showed up and he ordered another pint of Stella. The burger looked pretty good but the fries were frozen 'crispy' fries coated with that...whatever it was. At a seafood restaurant, on Edgartown Harbour, he didn't think that it was asking too much to get fresh cut fries. When and why did this French-fry coating become such a big thing? Oh well, something's got to give.

Talking to these JAWS 'FINatics' was a big part of Charles' life. They were artists, sculptors, factory workers, and grocery store clerks- every walk of life. It was wonderful. Somehow this story of a shark attacking a small east coast town had brought them all together. When JAWSfest was announced, they had all been on the various sites suggesting routes of transportation, offering to room with each other, and deciding when and where to meet up. When making the film, Robert Shaw would get drunk every day in Seasons Pub in Oak Bluffs. As a tribute, everyone who would be on the island on Wednesday had decided to meet at Seasons at 8:00pm. Technically, JAWSfest didn't start until Thursday but some were arriving the day before. Charles was one of the early arrivals and he was really looking forward to meeting his cyber-friends.

The ever-present seagulls ran, took off, dipped, swam, and landed. Whatever they had to do to get a morsel of food. More often than not, the cry of the gull was the only clear sound that you heard on the island. They were at their loudest on the harbour. There was a muddled din of voices, laughter, ship horns, and distant music but the seagulls were loud and clear. Charles finished his burger and left his fries. Under his plate he left sufficient cash for the bill and a healthy tip. Waiting tables was a tough job. Charles had done it and hated it; therefore, he always left a good tip. With a swig, he wiped out the last of his Stella and he was off to wander Edgartown.

4

The bus journey back to Oak Bluffs from Edgartown only retraced his previous trip but Charles welcomed it just the same. The sun was sinking and lighting the Atlantic Ocean afire with vibrant oranges and reds while Sengekontacket pond glistened quietly on the other side of the street. There were still people on State Beach but the JAWS Bridge had lost its jumpers for the day. Even Charles knew that he wouldn't be able to jump off the JAWS Bridge at dusk. Way too scary. Up Beach Road, the houses being built on the ocean side were skeletons against the bloodied sun. Charles inhaled the sea air deeply as he watched them go by. It had been a hot day and the sea breeze coming in the wide bus window was refreshing. Charles got off the bus in Oak Bluffs across the street from where he had gotten on earlier that day. He liked the feeling that parts of the island were now familiar to him and he looked forward to a time when he would feel familiar with the whole island but for now, he had to make his way with unsure steps into the business of Oak Bluffs to find Seasons Eatery and Pub.

Charles wasn't fond of downtown Oak Bluffs. It was the shabbiest part of the island and certainly not what he imagined in his head when he saw Martha's Vineyard. There were parts of Oak Bluffs that were lovely but the heart of the town was dirty and cheap looking. It was the city centres of Edgartown and Vineyard Haven that usually made the postcards and brochures because they were pristine and charming. Oak Bluffs was made up of sports bars, pool halls, video arcades, tourist shops, and seedy restaurants. The streets were loud and the people were raucous. The bars blasted music into the streets and there was a prominent police presence. There were cheap two-for-one T-shirts hanging in the shop windows and doorways. You could find souvenirs like ceramic lighthouses and mugs, ball caps, and shot glasses all for under $10. There was a place for that sort of thing and it would come in handy at the end of his stay but this was certainly not a part of the island that Charles wanted to spend any sort of time in. He would take the serenity of the rest of the island any day. Charles walked past the Flying Horses Carousel to take a left up Circuit Avenue but as he turned the corner he smashed head first into a cop carrying a coffee.

"*Jesus Christ!*" The officer looked down at the hot coffee now all over her newly pressed shirt. "What the *hell?* Watch where you're going!"

"Officer, I was!! I'm sorry but *you* weren't." Charles stood very still. Not sure what his next move should be.

"Oh...you're right. I wasn't... Sorry about that." She burst out laughing at her own clumsiness.

When the officer laughed, Charles became more focused and stared at her intently. "Laurie?" The officer looked up at him in shock at hearing her name. "Laurie Knickles?" He hadn't recognised her at first but that laugh was unmistakable. They had been best friends all through grade school and high school.

"Holy shit!" Her eyes lit up with realisation. "Charles Williams! I always wondered if I'd bump into you down here! I knew that JAWSfest would drag you in!! Am I right?" She smiled broadly.

"Totally! How could I help myself? But more the mystery is what the hell are you doing here?"

"I'm the Police Chief of Edgartown!!" Laurie beamed at her childhood friend.

"You're what?"

"I'm the Chief!"

"Wow! That's amazing! I'd hug you but you're covered in coffee," teased Charles.

"Yeah, no shit, and who's fault is that?" said Sheriff Knickles.

"You totally admitted that it was your fault!" Charles laughed.

"That was when you were a tourist; now, that you're a friend- I know better." She winked.

"You still haven't told me why you're the Police Chief here."

"How much time do you have? Where are you going?"

"I have to be at Seasons Eatery & Pub for 8:00 o'clock. Actually... I don't know where I'm going." Charles looked a little sheepish as he admitted that he was a bit of a fish out of water.

"You're not lost at all; it's right up the street here but hey, you've got a half an hour, come get a coffee with me and I'll fill you in. Cool?"

"Who am I to argue with the Chief of Police? I'd love it."

*　　*　　*

Charles sat at a table in Mocha Mott's just off of Circuit Drive. The line-up had been long but Laurie had assured him that it was well worth the wait. The place was tiny but it had a charm that was very much in line with the rest of the island. There was a hand made sign above the counter that read, "WE GO OLD SCHOOL HERE – PLEASE ORDER IN REAL SIZES - THANKS!!" Charles almost laughed out loud at the thought of these ladies being bombarded with mainland terminology like "venti", "tall", and "grande"- too funny. The folks on Martha's Vineyard really fought hard to keep the other world out and for the most part, they succeeded. Apparently, the line up at Mocha Mott's had been out the door and around the corner that morning. Just like a Tim Horton's back home in Toronto. Laurie came over to the table with their drinks and two little bags.

"What is this?" Charles asked when handed a bag. He peered inside. It was an apple fritter. How did Laurie know? It had been decades since they had seen each other. "Apple fritters are my favourite!!"

"Are they? Cool. I grabbed one for each of us. They are damned close to the world's best here."

"What would you have done if I didn't like apple fritters?"

"Sadly, eaten both of them." She sank her teeth into the dark brown pastry.

Charles followed suit. It was still warm and the sugar glaze melted beneath his fingertips. "Holy shit," he murmured with his mouth full of apple and cinnamon. "That's one serious fritter!"

"No kidding. I have to be careful with these things. My ass is going to get huge. Not to mention, it doesn't look good for a cop to be eating donuts all the time." She looked outside the window at the beautiful day they had abandoned. "You want to walk instead of sitting here? Let's go over to the park."

"That would be great." Charles laughed, "Maybe it's alright that you're eating it with a personal trainer!!"

Laurie looked at him and smiled warmly, "Maybe..." she paused. "It sure is good to see you."

"You too." Charles looked at his childhood friend and wondered how he hadn't recognised her right away. She hadn't changed that much. Sure, she was a little older but there were certainly no dramatic differences. Ash blonde hair with highlights, bright blue eyes, and a broad smile. She had kept in good shape too despite her self-deprecating comments. She must work out; Charles doubted that being a police chief in Edgartown was very physical.

The Seaview Park in Oak Bluffs was beautiful any time of day. Right now they were in the gloaming and the park, still warm from the hot sun, was filled with a yellow light. Well maintained, it was impeccably mowed and there were benches surrounded with the island's seemingly signature hydrangeas. There were couples on blankets, snuggled close, deep in private conversations. Kids were flying kites and being chased by parents who had far less energy than their children. The multicoloured Victorian homes that Oak Bluffs was famous for dotted two sides of the park and the other two sides were trimmed with beach. Charles and Laurie found a spot on a bench where they could watch the sun sink into the ocean. "So how did you end up here? Actually, let me rephrase that. How did you get lucky enough to work here?"

"You're right. That sounds better." Laurie thought for a minute before she spoke. "Remember that guy I was engaged to in high school? Well, I *dumped* him and started dating a very nice man named Mark, who was studying to be a doctor. We were married while he was still in school. He was a brilliant cardiologist." She smiled, lost in her memories. "While studying in Toronto, he was offered an internship at Massachusetts General. If you know anything at all about cardiology, you'll know that's like getting the Academy Award for that sort of thing."

Charles shrugged his shoulders. Cardio was heart- that's all he knew.

"Trust me." Laurie continued. "So he moved down here and after a lot of red tape so did I. To make a long story short, Mark did really well, we both got our citizenship, and I applied for the Boston police force. I was accepted."

"Where's Mark now?" If Charles had thought about it, he wouldn't have asked. There was no way the answer was going to be a positive one.

Laurie looked down at her coffee. "Five years ago, he was hit by a drunk driver. He died being wheeled into his own hospital." Laurie looked back up at him with dry but somewhat vacant eyes. "Is that irony? I was never sure."

"I'm sorry." Charles reached out for his friend's hand but she moved it away.

"No need. It wasn't your fault. I know what you mean though... Thanks." Neither one of them said anything for what seemed to be a very long time. "Mark did a lot of good in this world while he was here. What is it they say? The flame that burns twice as bright burns half as long? Something like that." The life returned to her eyes. "*I should have married that idiot from high school; he'll probably live to be a hundred!!"* They both laughed. "Anyway, after all of that, the city was too much for me. This job came up and I applied. I think they liked the idea of having a woman for chief. This is such a beautiful island. I remember you summering here when you were a kid. I always wondered what the big deal was. I sure get it now. Anyway, that's enough about me, what about you? What are you up to these days? Did you ever marry?"

"Me? No. I'm the eternal bachelor. I'll go on a couple of dates here and there but after about three...maybe four, people seem to think that they have control or they try to take precedent over the rest of my life and that really doesn't interest me. I'm always told, 'When you meet the right person, you'll change! It'll make a difference- you'll see!' but I'm forty-one now and I haven't met the right one. What's more, I don't care. I don't feel a void that has to be filled. I see these friends of mine, men and women, and they're lost if they're not in a relationship. Well, I say if there are people who feel lost if they're not in a relationship then there must also be people who are lost if they're *in* a relationship. You know what I mean? Balance in the universe and all of that other crap..."

"You're right." Laurie stared at him.

"I am?"

"Yep. *It totally sounds like crap!*" She laughed at sucking him in.

"Oh go to hell!" Charles laughed with his old friend. Sometimes there were people you could just pick up with after decades and it was like you saw them yesterday. "Oh shit! I should go."

"I should too. I need to get back to Edgartown and relieve my detective."

"So where am I going?" Charles looked toward Circuit Street to get his bearings.

"Come on, my car's that way; I'll walk you."

5

Seasons Eatery & Pub had a lot going on. There were bouncers at the front door as Charles walked in. What the interior design lacked in creativity, it made up in functionality. The large bar was crowded with a mixed group all enjoying the top forty, eighties hits pumped out at a decibel that made conversation almost impossible. Maybe that was why drunks were so loud? Maybe bars played loud music to cover up loud drunks, Charles thought, hmm...the chicken and the egg. There was a dance floor up front on the right that seemed to be in mid set-up for the evening's goings on. The bar itself, long, dark wood, with a brass rail buffer reminded Charles of the TV show 'Cheers' but that was a pretty standard design as far as bars go. Toward the back were tables and booths designed more for dining. They probably got a pretty good lunch crowd in here, thought Charles. It was way too noisy for a sit-down dinner but the lunch atmosphere was probably very different. There were flat screen TV's everywhere and neon beer signs. These, it seemed were responsible for most of the lighting. Behind the tables, it looked like there was a sushi bar?? Ok, that surprised Charles... only on Martha's Vineyard. It was toward the back of the room and in front of the sushi bar that he saw his friends. He headed in.

"HEY!" The first one to notice him was Jackie Lewis from Florida. "Oh my god!!" She ran toward him and wrapped her arms around his neck and gave him a big kiss. A very warm welcome for someone he'd never actually met before.

"Hi! Oh my god! This is so surreal!!" Charles had been talking to this group every day, sometimes more than once a day, for years but they had never met. He felt like he was at a high school reunion with people he'd never met.

After Jackie had yelled out and ran in his direction, the others had perked up. They were all beaming in his direction. He responded with the same wide smile. There were the identical twins, Mike Burroughs and his brother Sean, from Boston, Tim McKenna from Georgia, Andy Smith from Iowa, Larry and his sister Brooke Collins from England, and Eddie Simms and his wife, Tina, from Springfield. Which Springfield they were from, Charles had no idea. It seemed like there was a Springfield in each state to Charles. He thought there might be a law he wasn't aware of or something. "Charles!!!" Larry got up from his seat in a booth and made his way over to his friend. Larry was a good-looking man with almost black hair, blue eyes, and a square jaw. He had the trademark pale skin of the British and he was carrying the equally trademark giant stein of beer. "Good to meet you mate! Come have a pint!" Charles loved that Larry had called him 'mate'. Charles loved everything about the British. "When did you get in?"

"I got in around lunch. Just been hanging out; checking out the island. You know... What about you guys?" Charles was trying to greet everyone at the same time.

"It's brilliant to meet you finally, love!" Brooke, Larry's sister, grabbed his face with both hands and kissed him warmly. "Just brilliant. Isn't this the best? We got here yesterday. We're here for a whole week. If we're going to come all this bloody way, we'd better make the best of it, know what I mean?" Brooke led him over to their table to sit down and Larry had a chair under him just in time.

"What are you drinking?" Larry called the waitress over.

"What's that?" Charles motioned at Larry's large stein.

"22 oz of Guinness mate!"

"I'll have one of those."

Larry told the waitress to bring one for Charles and another for himself and to put them both on Larry's bill.

As the night went on, Charles learned that all of his friends were staying in Oak Bluffs. It was cheap and more of a party central. Charles had done his party thing. That wasn't what he was doing here. He wanted to savour every waking moment and he wasn't going to be able to do that with a hangover.

"Will you be at the opening ceremonies tomorrow morning?" Jackie was definitely feeling no pain. She was pretty and fresh looking with blonde hair to her shoulders and bright blue eyes.

"Definitely." Charles lifted his Guinness to his lips. The Irish stout was delicious. "I won't be going to everything but I figure that I'll wake up everyday and see what's what on the schedule. I didn't pay $300 for a VIP pass for nothing... at least, I hope I didn't!"

"You got a VIP? Alright!!" Tina held up her hand calling for a 'high-five' and Charles gave it to her. "That's the way to go!!"

"You too? Nice. Which Springfield are you from?" Charles asked.

Tina laughed, "Everyone asks us that. There are so many to choose from!"

Jackie looked at Charles, "I can't believe you got a VIP ticket. I guess you'll be up with all the big wigs."

"Are Tina, Eddie, and I the only ones with VIP's?"

There was a general nod of "Yep" and "Uh-huh" from the group.

"Damn, I wish I had known that. I'm probably going to end up sitting with you guys anyway. I could have saved the cash for my trip." Charles changed his tune, "Oh well! No regrets. I'm here and that's all that counts. This really is the best thing ever!! I can't believe I'm here!" Charles tracked down the waitress, which was no small feat, and ordered another round for everyone. It was a good crew and everyone was in high spirits. The last bus back to Edgartown wasn't for a few hours and Charles was going to make the most out of the night.

"Oi! Oi! Charles! Are you British?" Larry was leaning in over the table at him.

"No. I'm Canadian. Why?"

"You're the only fucker who's been able to keep up with me in the beer department!!" They looked down at their mugs; they were almost empty. "That's your second one! I'm impressed mate!!"

"That's a dubious honour at best!" Charles smiled. "It's somewhat of a family trait, I'm afraid. My background is Scottish and Welsh."

"Ah! That explains it then." Larry took a mouthful. "There will be more people coming in tomorrow but I think this is the gang of us for tonight. Not a bad lot. Are you a pool player?"

"I suck. I haven't played for years- like decades."

"That's rubbish mate! We're going to go play pool after this place. You should come anyway."

"I'll be heading back to Edgartown after here. I have to catch the last bus."

"Right."

"You assholes had better not be talking music without me!!" Tim from Georgia had swaggered over from his table.

"Oh Christ! Here we go!!" Larry slapped Tim on the back. "You've been waiting for Charlie to get here so that this could happen!! It's all you've talked about! This is supposed to be JAWSfest you know mate!"

"Not until tomorrow!! The three of us are supposed to talk music and that's what we're going to do! You're the first two assholes I've met, who even know who Dale Bozzio is! I'm not passing this up!!"

"You and Dale Bozzio! What's up with that?" Charles took his new Guinness from the waitress and gave her his empty mug. "She's cool and all but Debbie Harry is the real deal and no one is ever going to tell you differently!!"

"I agree." Larry chimed in.

"I'm not saying that Debbie isn't the shit; I'm saying that Dale didn't get enough credit. Nobody even knows who she is anymore. Debbie has her mark as a trailblazer and rightfully so. I'm just saying that Dale deserves her due." Tim was passionate on this and Charles knew how he felt. He didn't really see Dale Bozzio and or her band as being trailblazers but they were cool and probably should be remembered.

"Alright." Charles acquiesced. "I can see that." He lifted his mug. "To Missing Persons!"

"To Missing Persons!" They crashed their mugs together causing Guinness to spill over the table.

"Missing Persons? You mean the kids on milk cartons?" Brooke had come over to see what they were in such a huddle about.

"No, the band! See what I mean?"

"Never heard of them."

"I give up." Tim rolled his eyes.

"I heard that the guy who owns the salvage of the ORCA is going to be at this thing." Tim almost whispered this information as if you needed special security clearance to hear it. Charles' jaw almost dropped open. The ORCA? Charles thought that the homeless of Hollywood had long since used the iconic boat from JAWS for kindling. His interest had peaked to say the least.

"That's rubbish, mate! The ORCA is long gone." Larry's British accent rang out a lot louder than Tim, indicating that Larry didn't hold the information in as high regard. "Spielberg said that it had been tossed by Universal off of the back lot. They didn't save anything. It just rotted away."

"That's what I know too." Charles agreed. It made Charles sick when he thought about Universal just throwing out all of the major props from the movie. The sharks were thrown out and the boat, ORCA, was tied up on the JAWS Lake at Universal Studios. He remembered seeing it on a couple of episodes of 'Murder, She Wrote' when the JAWS Lake doubled as Cabot Cove. The last time Charles had seen a picture of it, it was sitting very low in the water. The hull must have been pretty much gone. It was so full of water. It rotted on that lake until there was no saving it...or so he thought. This story was new to him.

"I always believed the same thing but I heard a story recently that checked out with a couple of people. A friend of mine, who works at Universal Studios in L.A. and who was part of the JAWS crew, told me that the order to pitch the boat was given but this guy took it home instead of to the dump. There wasn't enough left to restore and make it functional but he's dried it out and has done his best to treat it, so that it won't rot anymore. Given it a lot of care; you know, like you would an old painting. Anyway, I've heard that he is bringing it here to unveil it. It's not even in the schedule but the idea of unveiling it here is pretty cool, don't you think? He could get bidding up with this crowd...if he's looking to sell that is." Tim seemed pleased with his captive audience and sat back. He smiled under his baseball cap.

"Why lug it all the way here if he's not looking to sell? Gloat? That seems pretty expensive for a dick move." Charles said. The FINatic in him was pretty excited at the idea, however incredible, of seeing the ORCA in real life. It would be wonderful to know that the iconic boat had been saved at least in part.

Tim sipped his beer. "Anyway, that's what I heard."

"I guess we'll all find out tomorrow."

"I guess."

"Even if the guy is a dick, I've got to give him props for swiping the boat. I've always been disgusted with Universal for letting all that stuff go. It would be awesome if that boat was still around let alone one of the sharks," said Charles.

"Agreed." The whole group seemed to nod their agreement.

"What do you think he could get for that boat?"

"Half a million easy."

"*Really?*" Brooke was astonished.

"Probably. I know the guy who owns the chair that Quint sat in on the boat and he paid over a hundred grand for it."

"How is it that he has the chair from the boat but not the boat itself? Who decided to take the chair off the boat and let the rest rot? That's moronic!"

"The whole thing is moronic." Mike and his brother Sean had been sitting peculiarly reticent and listening. Mike was largely considered the biggest JAWS fan in the world and his collection of JAWS memorabilia was always featured in pop culture documentaries. "The fact that Universal let things rot and gave things away, sold stuff for junk, is ridiculous. I bid on that chair but was out bid. That pissed me off. I got the harpoon gun and the barrels in separate auctions but not the chair. I'll get it when he decides to sell. There's no way that boat exists anymore. It's gone. If it still existed, I'd have heard about it. It's a wonderful thought though isn't it, Tim?"

"You really don't think it's out there?"

"No. No I don't." Mike motioned to the waitress to get a round for everyone on his credit card. "If I did,

I'd be out there hunting it down that's for sure. Even just to get to see it would be spectacular. I've exhausted every connection I have to find even a piece of her but found nothing. It's a sad story." Mike stretched. "Sorry guys! I didn't mean to bring everybody down. This is supposed to be a party! We can't be a bunch of drunks getting bummed out about a boat that rotted away over thirty years ago!! Get it together!!" Mike laughed.

"He's right," Sean, his brother, chimed in. "You're all taking this way too seriously!"

"Fine. Dale Bozzio vs. Debbie Harry?" Larry offered.

"No way! Been there, done that." Tim laughed.

"Human League vs. Spandau Ballet?"

"Now you're talking!!!" Charles lit up.

6

At 9am, Casey ran across the JAWS Bridge for the first time in his life. His parents had finally let him watch the movie the week before and he had loved it. He had loved sharks ever since he could remember. He watched Shark Week every year and had wanted to see JAWS for so long but his parents had always said that he was too young and it was too scary. When he turned thirteen, his parents asked him what he wanted and he had said, "JAWS!" His parents had given in. Casey got the JAWS DVD for his birthday along with a JAWS T-shirt and towel, and they had thrown him a JAWS birthday party; he invited some friends for a sleepover. His mom had asked each of the boys' parents if it was okay that their sons watch JAWS and they had all given their permission. His mom made a JAWS birthday cake and his dad made loot bags with a shark motif. His dad even made a "Pin

The Fin on The Shark!" game. It was way better than pinning a tail on a stupid donkey. They ate barbequed hamburgers and hot dogs and afterward they hunkered down to watch the movie. Some of the boys did get really scared and one boy asked to go home before it was over but Casey wasn't going to miss a second. He did get scared. The first bit with the lady getting eaten was really scary and he had jumped when that old guy's head popped out of the bottom of the boat but even though it was scary, he thought it was the best movie that he had ever seen. This year, to surprise him, his parents had brought him camping on Martha's Vineyard for vacation. What a bonus! Casey loved camping and he loved JAWS! This was the best summer ever!! When he was about halfway across the bridge, he climbed up the railing and looked down; it was a lot higher than he had expected. That was kind of freaky but he could do it. There were two other kids jumping off the bridge and he knew that people did it all summer. He climbed up onto the railing. The green water below was murky and moving at a pretty good pace. His thirteen-year-old body was skinny and long. His mop of sandy hair blew in the warm wind. He was nervous and his skin was covered in goose bumps. He stood there for what seemed an eternity. He jumped.

Casey splashed into the water. He went down pretty deep and as soon as he hit, he started kicking for the surface. His wild imagination conjured up images of a giant shark headed straight for him. Not just any shark- the JAWS shark. He knew it wasn't real but it made his heart beat so hard that his chest hurt and he wanted out of the water. Something felt wrong...very wrong. He broke the surface with a gasp and wiped the water from his eyes so that he could open them as soon as possible. They stung from the salt water but once they were open, he was relieved. No shark. No fin. He was panting but his heart rate seemed to come down a little. Casey was treading water almost immediately under the bridge. He felt something bump him in the back. Must have peddled back and hit the bridge itself, he thought...but it moved. Casey whipped around as fast as he could. The flesh that hit him in the face was bloodless and grey. It was unrecognisable as human at first but when a wave knocked the lifeless arm at Casey, he was slapped in the face by the dead man's hand. Grey, bloated fingers prodded his cheek. He started to scream. He inhaled a mouthful of water and choked. He flailed as hard as he could at the lifeless corpse. There was one eye in the grey bloated face and it stared at Casey accusingly. A black gaping hole was all that was left of the other eye. The flesh around it was ragged and fluttering in the water. Desperately, Casey tried to push the lifeless body away but the current kept smashing them together. He kept screaming...and choking. There was a head attached to the floating torso and one arm but not much else. It was a man. The body was scarred and shredded. Casey choked harder as he swallowed

the seawater. He could feel himself going under.
Everything went white before it went black.

7

Charles rode the number-thirteen bus home from Vineyard Haven. He had gone out early to have breakfast at the Art Cliff Diner. The Art Cliff was a small wooden shingle building with neat white trim and a brightly coloured sign on the roof. It was famous for its delicious food, friendly service, and celebrity clientele. He was told that Art Cliff got really busy on season and on weekends so it was best, if you didn't want to wait, to be there when it opened, promptly at 7:30am. It had been good advice. He got there at 7:25am and there were already people waiting to get in. The five-minute wait had certainly been worth it. Charles had ordered the 'Mr T Frittata': three eggs scrambled with Chorizo, jalapeno, onion, pepper jack cheese, and Tabasco served over layers of potato and toast. Delicious!! "That will put hair on your chest!" said the cheerful waitress when she brought his order to the table. Now, well sated, he found himself headed back to Edgartown.

The bus rolled along Beach Road up into Oak Bluffs where he had caught the same bus the day before. It stopped as scheduled, a couple of people got off, and quite a few got on. They were mostly islanders dressed for work. A couple of tourists got on with their beach chairs and picnic baskets, which they all stowed on the shelves behind the driver. Charles thought that was amazing. So many people got on with bags and bikes but instead of dragging them to their chairs like in Toronto, they would stow them on one of two shelves behind the driver and go and sit down. No one inconvenienced anyone with cumbersome packages and certainly no one worried about their things being stolen. It was a nice way to live- so civilised. With everyone settled, the bus started once again down its path on Beach Road.

As they got closer to State Beach, it seemed obvious that something was wrong. Traffic was lined up. Charles thought that there might have been an accident. The bus stopped and idled before rolling a little further and then idling again. It continued edging along until they got close enough that Charles could see out of his window that the police were indeed lined up at the side of the road. There were two ambulances there too. Quite a crowd had gathered but in the centre of it all, Charles could see his childhood friend, Chief Laurie Knickles. He pulled the bell on the bus and stood as the bus came to the stop for State Beach.

The beach was busy. The soft, cork coloured sand was peppered with brightly coloured umbrellas like push pins on a bulletin board. There were plenty of tanners around but there was no one in the water, not even children; this struck Charles as odd because you couldn't have asked for a better day. It was quite warm for mid-morning and there was a nice breeze but not one person was swimming. It really was like a scene from JAWS. Everyone was thoroughly engrossed in the goings on by the bridge. Charles walked over to the JAWS Bridge where the Chief was talking to her officers. As he got closer, Charles passed one of the two ambulances. There was a young boy in a bathing suit with an oxygen mask strapped to his face. His eyes were glossy and he seemed completely unaware of the two people, probably his parents, sitting with him. Physically, he looked okay though. There were no bandages that Charles could see. He realised that he was staring at the boy and quickly moved past. No one had noticed him but it was definitely a private moment and he blushed at his own intrusion. As Charles passed, the second ambulance drove off.

The Chief looked up in his direction as he got closer and motioned for him to stay where he was. Charles did as instructed and it wasn't long before Chief Knickles came over to him.

"What happened here, Chief?" Charles asked.

"You got a date?" Chief Knickles asked him.

"What do you mean?"

"Do you have somewhere you have to be right now?" She looked serious.

"No. Not really..." Charles had the opening ceremonies of JAWSfest in an hour but something told him that wasn't the answer that the Chief wanted to hear.

"Good. Come with me." The Chief led Charles over to her squad car and her officer caught up with her. "Jeff, can you go with the kid? I'll meet you there."

"Sure thing, Chief." Detective Jeff looked at him with a mildly inquisitive glance and hurried over to the ambulance where Charles had seen the young boy.

Charles and the Chief got in the car and she turned her key in the ignition. They pulled out of the crowd and drove off up Beach Road back in the direction of Oak Bluffs. "You're not going to believe this shit." Charles waited in silence for his friend to continue. "This morning a kid jumped off the god damned JAWS Bridge and found himself face to face with a half-eaten corpse!!"

"What!!" Charles had no idea how to react.

"You heard me. It's bad enough that I've got one of the busiest seasons that we've ever had; now, I have a thirteen-year-old boy assaulted by a half-eaten shark victim in the middle of JAWSfest!!" The Chief picked up her coffee and took a swig. She grimaced and Charles figured that it had been there for a while. "Jesus Christ! The press is going to have a field day with this not to mention all of your yahoo JAWS friends!" Chief Knickles drove the car up to Mocha

Mott's where they had been just the day before. She pulled a twenty out of her pocket and turned toward Charles, "Go in there and grab me an extra large latte and an apple fritter, would you? I haven't had any breakfast yet. Get yourself one too."

"No sweat but this one is on me." Charles opened the door of the patrol car without taking the money.

"Oh and don't say anything to anyone in there. It's going to be hard enough to try and keep a lid on this thing. I'd like ten minutes of peace before the shit hits the fan."

"Who am I going to tell?" Charles swung the door shut and walked toward the coffee shop. His mind was reeling- a shark attack at the JAWS Bridge during JAWSfest? That was bullshit. What was it that they said? The law doesn't believe in coincidence and science hates a coincidence? Someone, somewhere, said something like that. Charles made a mental note to look that up later. The more Charles thought about it, the more questions he had. A few minutes later he returned to the car with two lattes and two apple fritters. His hands were full and the Chief opened the door for him from the inside.

"The more I think about this, the more questions I have." Charles handed the Chief her food.

"No shit! Thanks for the feedback. It's like having Agatha fucking Christie for a ride-along!" the Chief looked at Charles. "Sorry. That was uncalled for.

You're quite right; it's mind boggling." She started the car again. "A helluva coincidence."

"I don't believe in coincidences." Charles stared out the window at the open ocean. It was calming, blue, beautiful, and endless; everything that an ocean was supposed to be. Was there really a man-eating shark swimming out there?

Chief Laurie Knickles smiled a half-smile and glanced briefly at her friend, "Oh yeah...I remember that." she tore off a piece of fritter with her fingers and popped it in to her mouth. "You never did believe in coincidences." She chewed her donut. "Why didn't *you* become a cop?"

"I have an aversion to being shot at." Charles washed down a piece of apple fritter with a mouthful of coffee. "Coincidence is nothing but smoke and mirrors." He stared out at the ocean. "It's usually just lazy people giving up before they find an explanation."

"That's crap. This could be a coincidence. A shark ate a tourist off the coast of Martha's Vineyard during JAWSfest leaving him to float up at the JAWS Bridge. Christ, that sounds ridiculous! That will be the headline though. How am I going to weave my way through that interview, I ask you?" The Chief kept driving.

"Where are we going anyway?"

"To the hospital. I want to see that kid. You don't have any official business here but you're seriously smart and I wouldn't mind having a sounding board that I don't have to be professional and politically correct with. I think better that way. This was not what I moved to the Vineyard for, I can tell you that." The Chief shook her head.

Charles was chuffed that his old friend had said that he was "seriously smart". Charles had been labelled a genius as a child with an IQ in the ninety-eighth percentile. The fact that Laurie had remembered that was very touching. He was very proud of it but also more than a little ashamed that he hadn't done more with his life. Now, in his forties, he felt that all the high IQ did was make him a bigger disappointment. It was nice to be acknowledged in such a positive light.

*   *   *

The Martha's Vineyard Hospital was impressive. Two storeys, red brick with white trim, and approximately 90,000 square feet, the building wasn't more than a couple of years old. Charles remembered reading on-line about the stages of construction in the Martha's Vineyard Gazette. It had been the largest undertaking by that particular construction company and that the basement mat slab of concrete alone had weighed more than 2.5 million pounds. Charles thought that was quite an astonishing build for an island hospital that serviced just under 15,000 residents off-season. Upon completion, the hospital had achieved an LEED silver rating- a rare feat indeed.

That had impressed Charles. Energy conservation and the environment were important to him.

The chief drove her car down Eastville Avenue, made a left back onto Beach Road and took the first left up to the emergency entrance. They parked and got out. The windows had been rolled up and the air had been on for the drive; Charles had forgotten how warm it was. There were no clouds for coverage and the sun beat down on him intensely. He made a mental note to put on some sunscreen when he got back to the car. He was always forgetting to put on sunscreen.

The emergency entrance was nestled between the main entrance and the ambulance entrance housed under an elegant, white porte-cochere with EMERGENCY written in large red print across the front. The automated glass door slid open as they approached and they were met by a blast of cold air. Charles welcomed it. A pudgy little nurse with a bun of grey hair sat at reception.

"Hi Chief!" The nurse welcomed Laurie with a familiar smile. It was a pretty sure thing that on an island of 15,000, it wouldn't take long before you'd know a good number of residents but being a Police Chief guaranteed it.

"Hi Connie. How's your day?"

She smiled, "Better than yours, I'd imagine. You here about that boy?"

Chief Knickles nodded.

"I figured. What a sweet kid. What a terrible thing for a little boy to go through." Connie shook her head sadly.

"Not very pleasant for an adult either." Chief Knickles said dourly.

"No, I don't suppose but *jeez-Louise* he's the same age as my grandson- breaks my heart."

"Mine too. Where is he Connie?" The Chief spoke with a pleasant tone but one that let everyone know that this conversation was over.

Connie would talk all day if you let her; Charles could tell.

"Just down to the left. You'll see Jeff outside the room." Connie smiled at them with an energy that made her age difficult to gauge.

The Chief looked down the hall and saw the officer standing outside a hospital room. The door was closed. She turned around to Charles. "Okay, you have a seat. The last thing in the world these people need is a tourist hanging out watching them- not right now anyway." Having said her bit, the Chief walked down the hall and Charles could see the officer stiffen slightly as she approached. They talked for a minute and then Chief Knickles knocked on the closed door and went in. The officer looked down the hall in Charles' direction. It was not a welcoming look. He took it as his queue to go and take a seat in the waiting room.

Charles pulled out his iPhone and surfed the Internet but it wasn't long before the Chief reappeared with the officer in tow.

"Okay, we can go." Chief Knickles motioned toward the deputy, "Charles Williams, this is Detective Jefferies. Jeff, this is one of my oldest friends, Charles." With the introduction, the detective's face lightened considerably.

"Oh! I've been wondering! Very nice to meet you Mr Williams." The detective grabbed Charles' outstretched hand and gave it a vigorous shake.

"No please, call me Charles." He reached out and they shook hands.

"I'm Jeff."

"Jeff?" Charles paused, "Jeff Jefferies? Really?"

The detective and the Chief both laughed. "No! Sorry, my dad is the Fire Chief; we're both Peter Jefferies. I became 'Jeff' for short. It cut down on the confusion."

"Oh! Your dad is the fire chief? That's pretty cool. Does he work out of Edgartown too?"

"Yes, he's been the Chief there for my whole life. We work pretty close together sometimes hence the confusion."

"He is an excellent Chief. I had to do some pretty fast manoeuvres to keep up with him." Laurie nodded in respect. "He was close with the last Chief. Comes around a fair bit. There are a lot of good people on this island." The three of them started outside. "Thanks Connie!" the receptionist waved a heavy arm at them as they left the building. "Jeff, I'm going to drive Charles wherever it is that he needs to go." She turned to Charles. "Where is it that you need to go?"

"The Old Whaling Church but you can drop me at the Edgartown Inn. I might have to pick up a few things."

"Fine. I'm driving him to the Edgartown Inn and then going back to the office. I'll see you there. Will you get the paperwork started on our John Doe for me please?"

"Sure thing, Chief. Good to meet you Charles; catch me off-duty sometime for a beer!" Detective Jeff walked in the opposite direction of the other two; all three headed towards their cars.

8

Charles walked into his guestroom at the Edgartown Inn in a state of bewilderment. It had been quite a morning! Not at all what he had expected when he had set out for his leisurely breakfast at the Art Cliff! How often do you go out for breakfast, discover that a man had been eaten by a shark *and at a JAWS filming location*, no less, and then drive with the police to the hospital to check on the boy who discovered the victim? If Charles had bumped into a shark victim while swimming at State Beach, he would have had a stroke! That was one tough kid. Charles wondered what kind of shark it had been. The Police Chief was probably waiting on the autopsy report but Charles was sure that if he got a look at the pictures from the crime scene that he could figure it out. He looked around the room for a phone book. He found it on the bottom shelf of the nightstand. After skimming through it for a minute, he pulled out his iPhone and dialled.

"Yes, hello. My I speak to Chief Laurie Knickles, please? Tell her that it's Charles Williams calling." Charles sucked on his lower lip pensively and furrowed his brow while he was placed on hold. "Hi Laurie. I was wondering if you had crime scene photos from this morning?"

"Yes, of course. Why?"

"Well, I thought that if you wanted me to take a look at them, I could probably tell you what kind of shark attacked the victim if that would help you at all. What do you normally do in a situation like this?"

"Well, first of all, there is no 'normal'; this situation is far from normal. You make it sound like we're dragging shark victims out of the water left, right, and centre around here; we're not. Procedure has us call in a shark guy from Wood's Hole and wait for the coroner's report to come back from Boston. That might take three or four days; however, I put a rush on this one so I'm hoping it won't take more than two."

"Oh, okay. Well, I just thought that I'd offer. I'd better go." Charles felt that he might have overstepped his bounds. Sometimes he got so caught up in trying to solve a problem that he forgot about the other people involved and what might be deemed appropriate.

"Whoa! Hold on there! I didn't say, 'no'! Jesus, you're touchy." Laurie chuckled. "I don't think that there would be any harm in letting you see the photos. You might be of some use. You are the closest thing to a shark expert that I've ever met. I'd love for one of those shark guys to come up here and think we have a clue- always a bunch of assholes. What are you doing now?"

"I'm on my way to the JAWSfest. I'm not sure what is going on at the moment but I'd like to go to part of it. I paid $300 for the damned VIP bracelet."

"*Of course* you did. Okay, I have a JAWSfest program around here somewhere. I'll come and pick you up in a couple of hours. Just stay at JAWSfest; I'll find you. Is that alright?"

"Yes. That's fine. I'll see you later." Charles hung up the phone.

Helping the police, as ghoulish as it sounded, was kind of exciting. He realised that this was a tragedy. A life had been lost and another had probably been permanently scarred but damn it- this was exciting! Charles had always loved Law & Order and CSI. To experience an investigation in real life was going to be very interesting. Right now, he needed to clear his head. If possible, put current events temporarily out of his mind; that would not be easy. He went over to the darkly varnished desk and got out his JAWSfest schedule. He had missed most of the opening ceremonies but there was a reception for attendees and VIPs being held at the Daniel Fisher House on Main Street. It was to be attended by locals who had been in the film and some people from the production who had flown in from Hollywood. That would be cool. A light lunch and cocktails were to be served and it was open bar to VIP bracelet holders. That sounded VERY interesting. Charles decided that he really wanted a pint. He could make it if he hurried. He went to the bathroom to wash up and left.

As Charles walked down North Water Street, he was deep in thought. His body was walking down the narrow sidewalk past The Kelley House but his mind was still on the drive back from the hospital. The boy, Casey Boyd, was fine, Laurie had told him. He hadn't seen any sign of a shark other than the victim. That was something. The doctors were keeping him in the hospital overnight for observation but they figured that he would be fine to go home in the morning. He had been given a mild tranquilizer; therefore, Charles figured, Casey would probably sleep pretty soundly. The Chief said that his parents were in worse shape than he was. That was usually the way it worked as far as Charles could tell. Kids are usually fine if their parents leave them alone.

The John Doe, what was left of him, was being shipped off to Boston for autopsy. As it turns out, Martha's Vineyard doesn't do its own autopsies. They outsource them. They wrap them up and ship them out like dry cleaning. Too bad they didn't get the same turn around time. It seemed odd to Charles but there probably just wasn't enough work to keep one guy busy throughout the year. Charles remembered seeing that there was an oncology department at Martha's

Vineyard General. They had *oncology* but no medical examiner or coroner? That was one hell of an oncology department, thought Charles. He smiled at his own tasteless but keen observation. Anyway, it would take a couple of days to get the results back from the mainland. Not that there was much to know. The tough part was going to be not telling the JAWSfest people about the attack. That was going to be big news to the JAWS folks. Charles began pulling open all of the filing cabinets in his brain that had any information at all about shark attacks. In fact, he almost passed Main Street. At the last minute, he woke up and headed up toward the Old Whaling Church and Dr Daniel Fisher House.

Main Street was beautiful. It started at the Edgartown harbour and rolled uphill and through the centre of town. It bisected Water Street into North and South and headed straight up into the heart of Edgartown. The interiors of the tiny shops on either side of the street had changed since Charles was there last but the edifices were the same. The same exteriors in 2001 as there were in 1981. They were probably the same since 1881, Charles guessed. The streetlights were no longer gas but they were still in the gaslight style. Black wrought iron poles with a diamond-shaped, glass encasement; except, where there once had been a flame, there was now a bulb. Each pole also had two hooks fixed to it on opposite sides with a hanging pot of red geraniums in each. It made for a lovely effect. The austere structure of the uniform white buildings with black shutters and lampposts brought to life by red and green geraniums and full green trees. The city was timeless and perfect. Charles passed the Edgartown Town Hall and knew that he wasn't far from his destination. The Old Whaling Church appeared in front of him and it was as impressive as Charles remembered. It was one of the most beautiful examples of Greek revival architecture that he had ever seen up close. The Old Whaling Church had been built in the 1840's. It was no longer a functioning place of worship but it was rented out for weddings and things like that. Charles loved it. The huge windows, the black double doors, white pillars, the peaked roof, all under a strong, white, square steeple that encased a black faced clock with gold roman numerals. It was a magnificent building. It would be a cool place for a wedding at that, thought Charles. You could have the ceremony in the main room and then the reception downstairs in the adjoining hall. Charles didn't know how many people it held- 500 at least, would be his guess. He knew that a lot of the JAWSfest lectures were taking place there and he looked forward to being inside for the first time after admiring it for so long. The town maintained it beautifully and with the exception of adding the wheelchair ramp to the front, Charles would bet good money that it looked exactly as it did the day it was built. Charles wondered if he could find pictures of its construction on the Internet; he would have to look that up later. Adjacent to the church was the Daniel Fisher House.

Dr Daniel Fisher had been the most successful whaling captain on Martha's Vineyard when the whaling industry was in its heyday. It showed in his home. Charles had read that the house had been built in the very early seventeen hundreds; that made it one hundred and forty years older than the Old Whaling Church even though they were both in the same Greek revival style. The two-storey house was white with black shutters and was trimmed with hanging baskets of red geraniums. Edgartown was nothing if not consistent, thought Charles. There was something to be said for consistency. It was 'T' shaped with the top of the 'T' running along Main Street. There was a main door on the west side of the home with a porte-cochere over the drive. The base of the 'T' jutted away from the street onto the expansive grounds. It was obvious that the back of the house was the kitchen and servants' quarters; it had much less ostentatious doorways and windows and a simple peaked roof where the main roof was flat, trimmed with a neatly carved rail, and had a widow's walk in the centre. The west side of the ornately detailed home held a beautiful lanai typical of the style and time that overlooked the lawn and the Old Whaling Church. Impressive white pillars framed the porte-cochere, the lanai, and the front door that had been used to receive formally invited guests when it was a residence and in fact, still did. A well-manicured lawn separated the Daniel Fisher House from the Old Whaling Church and there was quite a party going on. With the help of his VIP bracelet, Charles bypassed the line-up outside the Main Street door of the house and slipped inside. Membership had its privileges, smiled Charles.

Barricades had forced Charles to turn into the west parlour upon entering. It was filled with JAWS memorabilia that was kept at a safe distance from the fans by a thick burgundy rope and brass posts. Never underestimate the power of the rope, thought Charles. There were production photographs, dorsal and tail fins from the long lost mechanical sharks named 'Bruce', yellow barrels that had been harpooned into the fish in the movie, the harpoon itself complete with harpoons and green metal case, Quint's big game fishing chair from the ORCA, sculptures of the main characters, shark jaws, and JAWS themed artwork. Charles took his time looking around. There were pieces of the hull of the "ORCA 2" that had been sunk and un-sunk as production needed. An islander, who worked on the crew, had purchased that boat right after production closed while the original ORCA had been shipped back to Hollywood and left to rot. Charles made his way through the parlour all the while marvelling at the fact that he was in a 300 year-old home. He loved that kind of thing. History was so fascinating. He turned right and walked through what had probably been the dining room and made his way out onto the lanai. He had seen from the street that the bar was set up there.

With his first step onto the lanai, Charles noticed a lot of familiar faces of people that he had never met. Joe Alves- production designer of JAWS, JAWS 2, and director of JAWS 3-D, Lee Fierro- local actress from the film, Edith Blake- local writer and photographer who wrote 'On Location On Martha's Vineyard (The Making of The Movie JAWS)', Jeffrey Kramer- Hollywood actor from the film, Wendy Benchley- wife of novelist Peter Benchley who wrote the novel, and Carl Gotlieb- actor in the first film and screenwriter for the first, second, and third JAWS instalments. They were all there. Charles had never been an autograph kind of guy. He thought that it was very un-Canadian. There were a lot of celebrities in Toronto and they always said that they loved it there because they could go wherever they wanted and no one bothered them. Canadians thought it was cool to see a celebrity and would milk it for a good story over a fabulous restaurant lunch but they would never go up to someone and start talking to them and/or ask them for an autograph. It seemed so odd. Charles made his way over to the bar and ordered a vodka and tonic. He remembered that Laurie would be picking him up at anytime and he didn't want to be staggering through the police station reeking of alcohol. This was his one and only drink. He would sip it and since it was vodka, he figured that he'd be safe.

"Hey bro!"

Charles turned around to find the good-looking face of his JAWS buddy, Andy. "Hey man! What's going on? Where is everybody?"

"Oh, they're around. I broke from the crowd in the hopes of picking up. There's some hot chicks here man! There's a blonde with a nice rack that is totally into me man." Andy was grinning boyishly from behind a pair of black Ray Bans- very Tom Cruise circa 1983.

Charles looked around. "Well? Where is she?"

"Oh...uh...heh-heh, I kinda lost her."

Charles grinned his half smile and lifted his eyebrow- a look that he was famous for. It spoke volumes.

"No! Really! Kind of a cougar kinda chick. I dig that."

"What kind of chicks don't you dig, Andy?"

Andy laughed, "I hear what you're saying, man. Oh! There she is! Gotta go! The others are here somewhere." With that, Andy was gone- cutting through the sea of people with a mid-western erection like a schooner. He was a good guy. He'd settle down once somebody landed him.

Charles nursed his drink and mingled through the crowd. He had the pleasure of finding himself in a lovely conversation with Wendy Benchley about shark conservation and then a quick chat with Jeffrey Kramer about different roles that he had done other than JAWS and JAWS 2. It was then that he caught up with Mike and Sean Burroughs, the identical twins from Boston. Mike was the JAWS collector. Charles was happy to have a chance to speak with him. They had talked at length on-line but hadn't really had the opportunity at Seasons. "Mike! The display inside looks excellent! Nice work. Most of that stuff is yours isn't it?"

"Of course! There's a sign inside with my picture on it, didn't you see it?"

"No, I'm sorry. I must have missed it. I must admit that I didn't take as much time as I would have liked. I'm not sure how much time I have today." Charles checked his phone for messages at the thought of time.

"You should go back. There are some really interesting finds in there. Read my sign too. It gives a little bio on me and where you can see other parts of my collection." It was obvious that Mike took all of this very seriously. Sean, on the other hand, just stood beside him and drank his beer. He didn't seem interested at all.

"That's not all of it?"

"*What?* Not even close! Most of my collection is still at home but some major pieces are in California for the opening of an exhibit on Great White Sharks at The Monterey Bay Aquarium. It seems contraindicated to have a JAWS display at an aquarium but giving things a pop-culture flare helps draw in the crowds."

"That makes sense." Charles really liked Mike but he took this JAWS thing really seriously- a little too seriously for Charles. No one would believe that back in Toronto. "Well what you have here is very impressive. I don't see what else you could possibly get! Unless you got that junkyard guy to sell you that 'Bruce' or actually found the ORCA." Charles laughed but regretted it almost instantly.

"I offered that junkyard jerk a lot of money for Bruce and he turned his nose up at me. I wouldn't even have a problem with that if he took care of that shark but he doesn't! It's falling apart bit by bit! It's the last remaining shark designed by Joe Alves! Go ask him! He's right over there! Even Joe has offered him money and he built the fucking thing!!! Nothing. It's barely a shell. What's he holding onto it for?" Mike took a swig from his beer. "As for the ORCA, it doesn't exist. I've exhausted every scent on that trail and what's it got me? Nothing. The ORCA is gone. I wish people would leave that alone."

Charles stood there in awkward silence when his phone went off. It was Laurie. "I'm out front of the Fisher House."

"I'll be right out." Charles put down his drink on one of the side tables. "Well it was a real pleasure Mike. I hope you get some help."

"With what?"

Charles had never been so thankful to be called away. Walking back through the house, he bumped into the Brits, Larry and Brooke. "Oi! Where are you going?"

"Oh, I've been called away for a bit but I'll be back. I think. Man, that Mike guy is wound pretty tightly, isn't he? I mean, I like JAWS but holy crap…"

"Yeah, we noticed that the other night. I think it's all he's got- kind of sad. Means well enough though. Anyway, sod him. Are you going to be at the screening tonight in Vineyard Haven?"

"Wouldn't miss it but look, I really have got to go." Charles hurried out of the house and onto Main Street. He jumped into the Chief's squad car and as he was putting on his seat belt, he saw Larry and Brooke starring after him with shock and confusion. Great, he thought, how am I going to explain this?

9

"How was your party?" asked Laurie without looking at him.

"Spooky."

Laurie snorted, "Why?"

"I shouldn't say that, it was very nice. It's just that I guess these sorts of things bring out an odd element...like a comic book convention. Everybody was really cool but some people are a bit too obsessive for me."

"*Too obsessive for you*! I find that hard to believe. Unless you've changed dramatically over the years and I doubt that. You're at JAWSfest for Christ's sake! Hello, Pot? This is the kettle; you're black!" She laughed at her own joke.

"I know, I know. Maybe that's what freaked me out. Maybe they were just exhibiting qualities that I don't particularly like about myself. That's probably it. They're all really nice people. I enjoyed talking to most of them. There were lots of people from the production there; that was cool. I met Joe Alves, Wendy Benchley, Jeffrey Kramer."

"I don't know who any of those people are."

"Well, I met Lee Fierro & Edith Blake."

"Oh, well, I know them; they're islanders. What were they doing there?"

"Oh my god! You're such a loser." He looked at her in disbelief.

"What!" Laurie glanced at Charles quickly before returning her focus to the road.

"Fierro was *in JAWS* and Blake wrote one of the 'making of' books! How can you not know that? You're the Police Chief here!!" He was completely disgusted.

Laurie started to laugh. "Now who's obsessive?" she laughed even harder. "Of course I know that! It's crammed down your throat at every turn on this island! You get to know the local celebs pretty quickly around here. Just for the record, I know who Carly Simon is too!"

Charles couldn't help but smile. Had he really sounded just like Mike back there? Probably. Mike was probably over-tired and Charles was probably stressed from his morning at the bridge and hospital. "That was a dirty trick."

"Oh please, you would have done the same thing to me in a heartbeat. Anyway, I'm about to make it up to you."

"You are? I'm not sure I trust you."

"Trust me. You're going to love it. Unless I miss my mark completely but I think I'm right about this." The chief's black and white squad car turned into the drive of The Edgartown Meat and Fish Market. It was a single storey, L-shaped building decked out in the traditional weather worn shingles and white trim. The main entrance was in the elbow of the building and they pulled up right in front. The chief got out of the car. Charles undid his seatbelt and called out to her, "Am I getting out?"

"I would."

He got out of the car and looked at the sign again to see if he had missed something. The Edgartown Meat and Fish Market, it read. It still said the same thing. "You're going to buy me meat and/or fish?" He closed the car door. "It's a lovely gesture but you really don't have to do that."

"Will you shut up and come inside!" Laurie rolled her eyes, smiling.

Charles followed the Chief inside and his surprise hit him like Christmas in August. He stared at the familiar long brown counter in front of the wall-mounted, black chalkboards. He knew this all too well-local art on the walls, overstuffed leather furniture, wooden tables and chairs, coffee beans, the white disposable coffee cups, the brown paper sleeves and yes, the green mermaid. "STARBUCKS!!"

"Yep. Don't tell anyone."

"I thought you guys didn't have a Starbucks!!"

Laurie tilted her head back and forth, "Technically, we don't have a Starbucks per se... They won't let one on the island but where there's a will there's a way. The fish market has been licensed to serve Starbucks Coffee. Starbucks even came in and trained the baristas. How's that for a loophole?" She could tell that this had made Charles very happy. "What'll you have? It's on me."

Charles looked at the barista behind the counter. "May I have a venti, six-shot, non-fat, extra-hot, Americano Misto, please?" He rang it off like a pro.

Laurie looked at him in wonder and disgust. The only word that she had caught was 'please'. "A *what*? You want a what?" She looked at the teenager behind the counter who was writing on a green and white cup with a black grease pencil. "Did you understand that?"

"Yes ma'am."

Laurie shook her head. "Well then I'll have one too. Do you guys sell apple fritters?"

*   *   *

The Edgartown Police Station on Pease's Point Way was an impressive building. Of course it was decorated in the grey shingle, white trim style but the structure itself had a modern edge to it. It was a big building, almost barn-like. There was even a turret of sorts where a silo would be. Charles wasn't sure what that was about. There was a long wheelchair ramp up the front and, all things considered, the building probably stood a full three storeys high even though there were really only two floors. What made the building look a little odd were the windows. They were small for a building of that size and oddly placed... at least not traditionally placed.

Police Chief Laurie Knickles strode in the front door and was descended upon almost immediately by police officers with questions. She answered each of them with concise answers but never broke her stride. Charles got lost temporarily in the mêlée. By the time that they had reached her office, the crowd had thinned and Charles had to catch up. The last remaining officer waited while the Chief signed something for him and then he left, closing the door behind him as he had been asked. They were alone again.

The Chief picked up the phone, "Jeff can you bring in the photos from this morning please?" She hung up.

"How many officers do you have?" Charles took a sip of his Starbucks and savoured the familiar, strong, brown liquid. He loved being on the island but it was nice to have a flavour from home.

"Four Sergeants and Jeff, my one Detective." Laurie stated matter-of-factly. "A really great group. I was lucky. It could have been a real pain in the ass coming in here as an outsider. The Vineyard doesn't warm too quickly to off-islanders in a position like this. It could have been very dicey for me with Jeff being the Detective and the Fire Chief's son. A lot of people figured that he would be stepping into this position for sure. Between you and me, Jeff *will* be Chief someday but he just wasn't ready. It would have been setting him up to fail and that wouldn't have been fair to such a good cop. His dad sat him down and told him that. He also told him that I would need him so very badly when I stepped into this position and he was right. I brought a lot of police experience with me; I'm a good cop; that's why I got the job but I needed Jeff's Vineyard experience to make this work. Jeff saw that and checked his ego at the door. Everyone else followed his lead. I owe him a great debt." As if on queue, there was a brief knock and Detective Jeffries entered the room.

"Here are those photos you requested Chief. Hello again, Mr Williams."

"Charles, please! Good to see you Jeff."

"She took you to Starbucks! What's with you mainlanders? Mocha Motts and Dock Street Café have awesome coffee and lattés! We don't need Starbucks on Martha's Vineyard."

"Dock Street Café? Where's that?" Charles was listening intently now.

"It's right at the bottom of Main Street at Dock Street- not far from The Edgartown Inn at all. Check it out tomorrow morning. You won't be sorry." Jeff winked reassuringly.

"I'll give it a go. The Chief just brought me to Starbucks because she guessed that it's what I drink at home. She was right; however, the Mocha Mott's was excellent."

"Their fritters were certainly a damned sight better than these! What the hell is this? It's like glazed Styrofoam!" The chief chewed in disgust. "Never again. Yeesh..."

"That'll learn ya!" The Detective laughed good-naturedly. "Anyway, there are your photos. Do you mind if I ask what you guys want them for?"

"Well, Jeff, if I know anything at all about Mr Williams here, it's that he's more of a shark expert than anyone I've ever met in my life. I am going to ask him to take a look at these wounds and maybe give us an idea of what we're dealing with out there in the big blue sea."

"Oh!" The detective raised his eyebrows with a look of mild surprise. "You're an ichthyologist?"

"Strictly amateur, I'm afraid but if I can help, I'd be honoured."

"That's cool. Can I stay, Chief?" Jeff was tall and thin and all smiles. It made him seem younger than his years.

"Absolutely. Close the door." The Chief picked up the large manila envelope and slid out a pile of large photographs. She laid them out in the sequence in which they had been taken.

Charles stood up and walked around the credenza so that he could inspect the pictures properly. He said nothing. The two officers stayed quiet and glanced back and forth from Charles to the photos. He studied them carefully. They were all pictures of the scene at State Beach. Some were just the bridge and the rocks and some were of the victim. When he got to the close-ups of the corpse, he stopped and leaned in as close as he could until his face was about eight inches from the photo. His eyes slowly went over every inch of the grey, tattered flesh. There was skin, flesh, and bone. It was gruesome but Charles was lost in the details and didn't see the human being that had once been. He was looking at what wasn't there- the attacker. He needed to see what was missing in order to assess the perpetrator. He waited long and thought hard before he spoke. He wanted to be as sure as possible and he chose his words very carefully.

"Ok...see here?" He directed their eyes with his finger but didn't touch the actual photograph. "The flesh is shredded, torn. It's not a smooth cut. A tiger shark for example would bite cleanly not messy like this because it has serrated teeth. This shark did not. This outline here," he traced the jaw line of the shark on the victim, "...is quite big. It looks like this was the first hit. It was powerful-meant to immobilize. Also, there's not much left of the hip and there's barely a femoral head. That's very telling. It's not easy to crush a femur, that's a powerful shark. So going by size, strength, and technique, I'd say that this was a Great White."

"Of course it is. What with it being JAWSfest and all." The Chief sighed ironically and plopped down in her chair.

"Hey that's right! Probably came here for the festivities! Right Chief?" Jeff laughed.

"It's not funny, Jeff." She folded her arms grimly across her chest. "There's nothing funny about this."

Jeff stopped laughing. "Sorry."

"Are you sure, Charles?" The Chief looked up at her friend wondering how much she could rely on his word.

"Well, I'm as sure as I can be. My word's not going to stand up in court or anything but for my money, a Great White did this." Charles looked at the photos again. It was obvious that something had caught his eye.

"What is it? What do you see?" The Chief and the Detective both stepped a little closer to look at the picture that Charles had in his hand. It was the full shot of the victim- barely one hip, one full arm, one eye.

"Well, it might be nothing..." Charles was deep in thought.

"What!" The Chief glared at him in astonishment. "What do you see?"

"Do you have a computer that I could use?" Charles set down the picture carefully and went over to the Chief's desk. After the Chief logged on, she got up and let Charles sit in her chair. He turned to face the computer and started typing. Soon he found himself on the JAWS Facebook page. Quickly he started scanning through the group members, Mike Burroughs, Larry Collins, Brooke Collins, Tim Oakes- was that him? Charles clicked on his profile but closed it right away- wrong guy. Andy Smith, Eddie Simms, Tim McKenna, he kept going until he found the one he wanted- Karl Bass. "What do you think?"

The Chief went back over to the credenza, picked up the photograph and brought it over to the computer. The man in the Facebook profile picture was good-looking in that tan California way. He had short brown hair; he was a little heavy but not much. There was a big difference between that Facebook picture and the one in the Chief's hand but it was undeniable- it was the same man. "Karl Bass...Well, I'll be damned."

10

The sun was bright in Charles' bathroom. He loved a mid-day shower. It refreshed him in the summer and warmed him in the winter. Regardless of the time of year, it always seemed to give the second half of the day a new start. The shower in his room was in a square tub. It was very different but nice and roomy. The water pressure was perfect for Charles; it was a little on the hard side. He was a big man, so he found the heavy pressure almost therapeutic. It helped him think. Karl Bass. Charles had enjoyed conversations with him on Facebook and not that long ago. Of course, you can't tell too much from an on-line relationship but basically he had seemed pleasant enough. They had talked about movies mostly. That had been Karl's profession as well as his passion. Not too many people were lucky enough to be able to say that. After leaving the police station, Charles had come back to the inn and sat on the front porch with his laptop. The inn didn't have Wi-Fi but he found that if he sat on the lounge chair at the north end of the veranda, he could pick up the Internet from The Edgartown Library next door. He had spent a long time reading up on Karl Bass. Charles read his entire Facebook page and found him on a couple of other websites. There was quite a bit to learn about someone on the Internet especially, as it turns out, if you have a career in the entertainment industry. The Internet Movie Data Base, IMDB, had seen to that. That was, by far, the most comprehensive website that Charles had ever come across. Anyone, and everyone, who had ever done anything was on that site. Turns out that Karl had worked with Universal for a great many years and his first production had been JAWS. That was probably why it held such a special place in his heart. Karl was a true islander, born and raised on the Vineyard, who was hired by Joe Alves to do some wiring for the company. Karl and that other guy, Oakes, ended up going back to Los Angeles with the crew and making a good living there. That was why Charles got them confused, they both worked for Universal. Now Karl was dead. Had he come back to the island with the festival in mind or was he just visiting relatives? Did he even still have relatives on the island? Most islanders' ties ran pretty deep. Families had been there for generations. If he had come back for family, it would be easy enough to find out.

The Chief had mentioned going up-island the next day to Menemsha to talk to some fishermen about shark sightings. Charles had asked to go along. He thought that it might be very interesting to talk to a real fisherman about a great white! He hoped that it wasn't in the plan to kill the fish. The Chief had said that it might not be up to her. Once the word got out, there was nothing that she would be able to do about locals and summer dinks hightailing it out to sea to catch the 'monster shark'. The fishermen wouldn't take too kindly to a shark messing with their livelihood. Not to mention that for a tourist, killing a Great White was a pretty great story to take back to the big city and tell all your friends. It was sad but Charles knew that she was right. Big game fishing was a popular sport on the east coast and if there was a Great White in the water that had supposedly injured a bather then the chances of catch and release were slim to none. A lot would rely on how the media dealt with it. Commerce would favour sensationalizing the story but politics would favour downplaying it. When Charles had left the police station they still hadn't heard from the papers but it wouldn't be long. He was expecting big headlines in the morning. Commerce usually won.

Charles stepped out of his shower and grabbed one of the clean, white towels that had been placed for him in his room. It smelled fresh. He dried off vigorously while looking out the window. His main floor room looked directly down North Water Street. It was surprisingly quiet. There was a lull in the hustle and bustle as people had gone in to prepare for supper. The sun was bright and starting to set. Was it always perfect on the island? Charles imagined how wonderful it would be to be on the Vineyard in the rain and decided that, yes, it was.

There was a screening of a JAWS documentary in Vineyard Haven at 8:00pm. He sorted through his clothes and decided on a pair of green khaki cargo shorts and a white polo shirt. He also grabbed his denim jacket. It would be cool by the water after the sun went down, especially if he was just sitting on the grass watching a movie.

*   *   *

Charles stepped off the bus in Vineyard Haven in the same spot that he had been that morning on his way to Art Cliff Diner. It seemed like weeks ago. A lot had happened since then. He sincerely hoped that his evening would be less eventful. It would almost have to be. The walk from the bus station to the park where the screening was to take place was only a short distance. The sun had all but set and the shops were closed. Main Street was quiet. Charles headed north past Bunch of Grapes Bookstore. The screening was at Owen Park. He had never been there before so he wasn't exactly sure where he was going. Vineyard Haven was lovely. It seemed more modern than Edgartown but yet certainly more civilised than Oak

Bluffs. The school of thought was that down-island, Edgartown, Oak Bluffs, and Vineyard Haven, was more hustle and bustle while up-island, Aquinnah, Chilmark, Menemsha and West Tisbury, was quieter, calmer, and more private. Even though Vineyard Haven was down-island, Charles saw it as a hybrid of the two. It was a nice place.

Owen Park was a long narrow strip of manicured land that ran from Main Street down to the water. The Owen Park Beach was at the foot and the Tisbury Town Harbour Master House was about halfway down. Charles had never really sorted out the Vineyard Haven/Tisbury thing. He thought that Vineyard Haven was in Tisbury or West Tisbury but he wasn't sure. How was it that the Tisbury Harbour Master was in Vineyard Haven if West Tisbury was up-island and Vineyard Haven was down-island? He wasn't even sure if Tisbury and West Tisbury was the same thing; he'd have to look that up later. There was a screen, a stage, and a table set up half way down the park in front of a permanent gazebo. He still had about 30 minutes before the show was to start. Charles walked down to the water and pulled out his camera. It was dusk. There was no sign of the actual sun but there was still quite a bit of light and it was casting great shadows over the beach and the boats in the harbour. He started taking pictures. Kayaks and canoes were piled on the beach and boats moored off shore. Sheds on the dunes were picturesque, surrounded by high beach grass. He kept clicking his camera. When it was time, he walked back up to the screen set up in the centre of the park. A crowd had grown in his absence and he looked around for a place to sit. A group of people were waving for him to join them. It was the gang from Seasons; he smiled and headed over.

"Hey!" Andy from Iowa grabbed him and pulled him down to the ground with friendly exuberance. "What have you been up to all day man? Did you get hauled away in a squad car this afternoon? That's the fuckin' rumour dude!" Andy patted him on the back and then opened up his gym bag. He pulled out a beer. "Want one? I have a shit load, dude." Andy grinned like a high school kid smuggling alcohol into the prom.

Charles chuckled and figured that it was time to lighten up a little. "Sure. Thanks Andy." He took the beer and twisted off the top. He put the cap in his pocket. Charles was dead set against littering. Littering should have a prison sentence as far as he was concerned.

"Nice!!" Andy was pleased to have a partner in crime.

"How'd you make out today with the blonde?"

"Pretty good. She said that she would meet me at Seasons tonight; we're all going there after the show. You coming? You should totally come dude."

"Alright. I'm in."

"Nice!"

"What's this sod talking you into now? You got to watch him!" Charles turned around at the sound of a British accent. Brooke and Larry were sitting right behind him. He hadn't noticed.

"Alright, alright, I was only inviting him to Seasons with us tonight after the show." He handed Brooke a full beer as she handed back an empty bottle. He turned back to Charles. "The Brits tell us that they saw you getting into a cop car this afternoon at the reception. Is this true? Are you a cop, dude? You can't be a cop; you're not a cop, are you?"

"I am not a cop. Relax. I don't even think that drinking in the park is legal so if I were a cop, I couldn't be doing this. Besides...I'm from Toronto." He took a mouthful of beer. "I'm out of my jurisdiction."

"Oh yeah, right! Toronto! I gotta go there sometime. They have hot chicks there, don't they?" Even as he spoke, Andy was scanning the crowd.

Charles laughed at his friend's single-mindedness. It was refreshing actually. Andy seemed to be the only one at JAWSfest who was on the island just to get laid. "One or two."

"Shut up, Andy. Why did you get into the cop car, Charles? Is everything alright?" Brooke took his hand and looked genuinely worried.

"Everything's fine. Relax. The Police Chief is a very good friend of mine- that's all."

"Really? That's pretty cool." Larry looked impressed.

"Yes, I guess it sort of is. Where is everyone else?"

"There are a few around." Larry started pointing at people that Charles could not see. "Mike and his twin brother, Sean, are over there talking to Carl Gotlieb. I think Mike is asking him to sign something; he's interviewed Carl a bunch of times." He looked around. "That's Tim over there. I'm not sure what he's doing- HEY TIM!!"

Charles lurched back when Larry yelled; he hadn't been expecting it. He looked across the park in the direction that he had shouted and sure enough, there was Tim sauntering his way through the crowd. Charles had really enjoyed his conversation about music with Larry and Tim the other day. They were good guys.

"Hey Charles. What's goin' on?" Tim was very laid back. "It's a good crowd, isn't it? Almost time for the show to start. I heard you're a cop or something. Is that true? That's pretty crazy." He was one of those people who nodded while he talked like he was agreeing with everything that he said.

"We've already covered that, ya tosser!" Larry leaned over Charles' shoulder. "He's not a cop but his best mate is the Chief. Gotta make him a handy guy to have around!" Tim patted him on the back a little harder than necessary. "You need another bottle, mate!" Before Charles could argue, there was another bottle of beer in his hand. He had to admit, the beer was going down pretty smoothly. It was really cold. Temperature was everything with beer.

The emcee, a petite, mature, blonde walked to the microphone and began to speak, "Good evening everyone, for those of you who don't know, my name is Rebecca Thompson. Thank you for coming to the JAWSfest screening of "Sharks and the Environment." There was polite applause before she continued. "I would also like to thank our panel for being here. Mr Gotlieb, Mr Kramer, and Mrs Benchley, thank you very much for your time." There was more applause. "I would also like to mention all of those working behind the scenes to bring JAWSfest to you. There are too many to mention but as chief co-ordinator, I can tell you that a lot of hard work has gone into bringing JAWSfest to you. I hope you enjoy it. The panel will be available for questioning after the film, so without further ado, 'Sharks and the Environment." The film started and Charles' mind began to wander. He was brought back to reality when Mike and Sean came over to the group.

"Check it out!" Mike spoke in an excited whisper to Charles and the gang. "Carl Gotlieb signed my first edition of The JAWS Log *and* my 1974 original poster. I actually think that he was a bit hesitant at first- I really think he was but when Jeffrey Kramer said, 'Sure!' then he jumped on board. That Jeffrey Kramer sure is a cool guy. So friendly!" Mike had to stop to catch his breath. Charles was trying to merge this version of Mike Burroughs with the angry Mike Burroughs that he had met that afternoon. He was kind of child-like, emotionally immature; everything was an extreme. Sean on the other hand was quite reserved, almost stoic. He stood calmly behind Mike and his emotionless face was actually quite handsome. Sean took his brother's pause as his opportunity to speak.

"Mike, man, I'm going to take off. I don't care if I see this film and you know that you've heard all of the same questions over and over. I'm outta here. I'll see you back at the hotel." He waved at the group in a very non-committal way. "Mañana!" He was already walking away. For identical twins, Mike and Sean seemed to have very little in common. They probably did look identical in photographs but in person, they were very different. Mike was bounding with endless energy while Sean was lethargic to say the least.

"I take it he's not a JAWS fan?" Charles looked at Mike, who was already pulling plastic bags out of his gym bag and delicately placing his newly signed treasures inside them.

"Not even a bit. I don't know what's wrong with him." Mike shook his head vigorously. "He is totally sucking the life out of my trip. I'm glad he's gone. I'm certainly not bringing him back next time. All he wants to do is cruise the bars in Oak Bluffs and get laid. That's where he's going now- guaranteed he's headed off to Seasons or Nancy's."

"I should hook up with him later." Andy whipped around at the mention of women and watched Sean walking off in the distance. "Seems cool."

The people sitting around them asked them to be quiet and the group pretty much settled down after that. They all seemed to focus on the film but Charles' mind was far away. He was staring directly at the screen but it was the last thing that he saw. All he could see were details of the crime scene photos that he had seen that morning and the details of Karl Bass' life. Charles moved over to the side of the crowd and lay back on the cold grass. The sky was full of stars. Why was Karl on Martha's Vineyard? He hadn't checked in at any of the JAWSfest functions that Charles knew about. Someone would have mentioned him for sure. They all knew him. He stared at the stars and looked for constellations; Hercules was there and that meant that straight down from him was Scorpio. Tomorrow, Charles would ask the organisers if they had crossed Karl off of their bracelet registration sheets. If he had been there, someone would know about it. Over from Scorpio but slightly higher was Libra and a little further in the same direction was Virgo. In the opposite direction was Dolphinus- Latin for Dolphin. That was one of Charles' favourites. The Greek god, Poseidon, had wanted to marry Amphitrite but she had fled to the Atlas Mountains. One of the searchers Poseidon sent out was the dolphin; he had found her and persuaded her to marry. In gratitude, Poseidon, placed an image of the dolphin among the stars. Charles wondered if the Chief had found Karl's relatives on the island. That would be a good place to start. Someone had to be told that Karl was dead.

Charles drifted off to sleep, dreaming of sharks and dolphins.

*   *   *

"Oi mate! Wake up! Your bleedin' snoring and all!" Larry was shaking him at the chest. He had really been out.

"Sorry guys. Jesus. I was really out of it. Today must have really wiped me out!" Charles sat up slowly.

"That's alright, love. You didn't miss much in the film- same old, same old. It was lovely though, I enjoyed it; I'm glad I came. You still coming to Seasons?" Brooke looked at him hopefully but she knew what the answer was before she was finished the sentence.

"I'd love to darlin' but I'm wiped." He yawned.

"Yeah, you look pretty knackered. Go home and get a good sleep. We'll have a blast tomorrow."

Charles stood and stretched. The night had cooled off and he was glad to have his jacket. Then again, maybe that was just from sleeping on the ground. He said his good-byes and started walking toward the station. The bus came almost immediately after he got there and he started the seemingly endless ride back to his bed. The bus drove up Beach Road on its way back through Oak Bluffs the same way that it had come. The night air was fresh and felt good on Charles' sleepy face. They retraced their steps back to Edgartown. The bus really seemed to be taking advantage of the clear night roads. Maybe this was the driver's last lap, thought Charles. They pulled up in Edgartown at the bus stop on Church Street and Charles decided to walk the long way home despite his exhaustion. Main Street was quiet and the shops were dark. There was nobody on the sidewalk except for the occasional couple walking romantically, hand in hand. The lantern style streetlights burned an amber glow across the streets and the entire scene looked ethereal like a dream. Turning onto North Water Street, Charles could see the unmistakable flash of police cars in the distance. The cars weren't moving but there was a cluster of them. Lights flashed off of the neighbouring buildings like Fourth of July fireworks but with an incongruent silence. As he got closer, he could see that they were right in front of The Edgartown Inn. The Kelley House was a beautiful hotel and it was made up of a group of buildings. They were very much in keeping with the style of the rest of Edgartown. The main building sat on the south side of Water Street sprawling all the way down to the docks. The famous pub, The Newes From America, was nestled in the corner of the main floor. Charles loved that pub. He had eaten some delicious meals there and hoisted many a pint. He had never stayed at the actual hotel but once, as a boy, he had come in lost and needed the services of the staff and they had been so accommodating, even though he wasn't a guest, that he had never forgotten it. The rooms at The Kelley House were all in satellite houses: The Garden House,

The Wheel House, The Chappy House, and The Court House. The Chappy House and The Court House were on North Water Street directly across from The Edgartown Inn. Charles could see now that there was an ambulance as well. He felt sick to his stomach. This was a bit too much like the morning's incident for his taste. He just wanted to go to bed and it was right there! On the wraparound porch of The Court House was a man, crying. Charles recognised him right away- it was Mike Burroughs. He was sitting on a wrought iron bench in front of the hotel in the middle of the fracas. He was alone. Charles went down to the bench and sat down beside him. Mike was bent over with his hands in his face and didn't notice him. Charles took a deep breath before opening his mouth. "Mike! Jesus Christ buddy! What's the matter??"

Mike looked up at him with blood shot eyes. He was wide-eyed like a child and seemed very far away. He was shaking. They stared at each other for a long time. It was as if Mike could barely wrap his head around what he needed to say. Charles knew how he felt. It was as if he didn't say it out loud, it wouldn't be true. It couldn't be true. Both of their faces flashed red in the glow from the lights on the squad cars. They were sitting very close to them and Charles noticed that he could hear the lights click as they flashed. Mike finally spoke, "Sean's dead! My brother- he's been shot!"

11

"I'm starting to think that you're bad luck." The Chief of Police, Laurie Knickles, came out of The Court House directly behind the bench where Charles and Mike were sitting. Charles stood up at the sound of his friend's voice and turned around.

"Oh, hey... Yes, I'm starting to wonder that myself." Charles looked down at his shaken friend and back at the Chief. "Is this true? Sean's been shot?"

"*Sean*? You knew Mr Burroughs?" The Chief motioned to Mike sitting on the bench who had dropped his face back into his hands at the mention of his brother's murder. "You know *this* Mr Burroughs?" There wasn't a hint of a smile on the Chief's face.

"Oh well, yes and yes." Charles looked down at his pitiful friend bathed, as they all were, in the flashing red lights from the cruiser. He had just lost his brother- his twin at that. That must be devastating, thought Charles.

"Of course you do." The Chief walked around in front of Mike. She motioned across the parking lot to one of the EMS technicians standing by the ambulance on Water Street and they started over. "Mr Burroughs?" She crouched down in front of him and spoke very calmly and soothingly. Something that Charles had never seen her do before. "Mr Burroughs, I can't imagine how difficult this is for you. I'm going to need to ask you some questions because I will need your help in finding out what happened to your brother, Sean." She reached out and took his hands in hers. "But right now, I'm going to ask you to do something for me. I want you to go with these gentlemen, here, in the ambulance, all right? Would you do that for me, please? You need to go to the hospital and get checked out. They'll give you something to calm you down, have a doctor look you over, and when I get there, we'll have a talk. Ok?" Mike nodded vacantly and the EMS technicians guided him gently into the ambulance. They closed the back doors and, in a matter of minutes, they were off. Charles and the Chief watched in silence as it drove away.

"*What the hell* is going on around here?" The Chief looked back at Charles as if she expected him to have all of the answers. The Chief's lights were still flashing but the ambulance was gone. It was calmer now on the porch; there was only the two of them.

"How the hell should I know? I don't know what happened! I can't even figure out how Mike got back to Edgartown before I did."

"Apparently, he drove. That was as much as I got out of him though. When was the last time he saw his brother alive? That's what I'd like to know." Laurie was wincing from the light from her squad car. She walked over to the open door, reached in, and turned it off. She shut the door as quietly as she could, mindful of the late hour. Other than the two of them, North Water Street showed no signs of life.

"Oh, well, I think I know the answer to that."

"Of course you do. When was it, Sherlock?"

"At Owen Park around eight o'clock."

This information seemed to placate the Chief somewhat. Her face relaxed a little, as did her tone. "How do you know this?"

"I was there. Mike was talking to me when Sean said that he was going to leave and he did. We watched him walk away."

"Do you know where he went?" The Chief was deep in thought now mentally putting a picture together. She sat down on the porch steps and Charles sat beside her.

"Not for sure but Mike said that Sean had spent his entire time on the island trying to get laid. He said that he could guarantee me that Sean was going back to Oak Bluffs to pick up women at Seasons or Nancy's. A bit of a dog apparently."

"Was he very successful, do you know?"

104

"No idea. I really didn't know him that well. He was nowhere near as animated as his brother. He wasn't even a JAWS fan. He just came here with Mike. He barely spoke to us. Anytime he was at a JAWS event he looked really bored."

"You didn't see him argue or fight with anybody then?"

"Just Mike and that was just typical brotherly animosity- nothing extraordinary." Charles looked up at the Kelley House. "Who found him?"

"His brother- about thirty minutes ago, which leaves us, according to you, about a three hour window. I need to find out what happened in those three hours. You want to have a quick look upstairs? You might be helpful. You might see something."

"*He's still up there?*" Charles stared at the Chief in shock.

The Chief shook her head. "He's long gone. The medical examiner will have him OPD at the hospital."

"What's OPD? I thought that you didn't have a medical examiner?"

"Sure we do. Who told you that? It stands for Officially Pronounced Dead."

"Oh. No one told me, I guess... but you send your bodies out for autopsy."

"Not everyone needs an autopsy. We can pronounce here and then ship them out for autopsy if need be. We have to have a medical examiner." She shook her head. "So now that's settled, do you want to come and have a look?" Laurie looked at Charles

105

knowing full well what the answer would be. Charles wanted to see anything that he hadn't seen before- always had.

"Yes, I would actually."

*   *   *

Charles stepped into the room at The Court House and his first thought was that it was lovely. Everything about the place was elegant. The delicate muted gold and cream striped wallpaper, the dark wood furniture, crisp white sheets, and the navy chair and carpet, all made for a very elegant guestroom. Everything looked new without a trace of wear except for the place on the bed where Sean's murdered body had bloodied the corner of the sheet and pillowcase beneath him. It was grotesquely out of place with the rest of the room, thought Charles. Everything was so spotless. The Burroughs brothers were very tidy. Their clothing and souvenirs were stacked in neat piles on the desk and on the luggage rack provided. From almost any angle you could take a picture for the hotel brochure as long as you missed the half of the bed that was covered in gore. There was some spatter on the walls and sheets that surrounded the pillow but most of the blood had been absorbed into the pillow itself. Charles walked over to the bed and leaned over the pillow. He inhaled deeply. He thought for a moment and then looked around until setting his sights on a chair in the far corner. "May I stand on that?"

Laurie looked around the room. The chair was on the opposite side of the room from the bed. There was nothing on it belonging to either of the brothers and it was too far away to have any blood on it. "Knock yourself out. Just don't disturb anything more than necessary."

Charles stood up on the chair just as Detective Jeffries walked in. "Whoa! What's going on in here?" Jeff looked up at Charles on the chair and over to the Chief who stood by the bloodied sheets.

"Charles is just having a look. Give him a minute." The chief motioned for the Detective to stay in the doorway. The two policemen watched Charles in silence as he looked down on the room from his position on the chair. After a couple of minutes he hopped down.

"What was that about?" The Detective asked.

"Blood spatter, Jeff. I'm just trying to get a bullet trajectory. You should always look down for an accurate assessment; otherwise, you're only getting two-dimensions and you'll be way off. Anyway, this is just a speculation." Charles got down and walked over to the desk and looked in the trash. Then he got down on his hands and knees and looked under the bed. Standing up, he walked over to the closet. With a tissue on his hand to avoid fingerprints, he opened it by pulling at the top corner of the door. The closet was empty. He closed the door and went over to the clothes piled neatly on the top of the luggage rack. There was a gym bag beside the luggage on the desk that Charles recognised as Mike's. It was the one that he had put his JAWS memorabilia in. The pile on the luggage rack was Sean's. On top was a jacket that Charles had seen Sean wearing that night. It had been carefully laid across the folded clothes. He opened up one of the pockets and looked inside. "There's something in here. He wore this tonight. I saw him in it."

Laurie walked over and pulled out the piece of paper. She unfolded it. It was a receipt from Nancy's in Oak Bluffs. "It's a credit card receipt. Definitely for more than one person."

Charles looked around again. He focused on the bed and then looked to the bedroom door where Jeff was standing. "You have professionals coming in to go over all this?"

"On their way." The Chief nodded. "Thoughts?"

"Well they'll tell you for sure of course but Sean did get lucky...for a while at least. There's semen in the wastebasket. Probably used to be a condom in there; somebody removed it. The pillow and the closet both smell of the same perfume. Whomever he slept with hung her coat up in there. She might have been the murderer. If she was, she did it on her way out. I think that Sean was asleep when he was shot. The blood spatter indicates no fight or fall on his part. He was lying in bed already. My guess is that he was asleep. So, she either did it on her way out or the killer saw her leave and snuck in. The murderer shot him from the doorway."

"Very interesting. Thank you." The Chief looked at Charles and smiled for the first time that night. "I had a couple of similar notions but confirmation is always good. I didn't figure that he was shot from the door nor did I smell the perfume. I suspected that was semen in the garbage; we'll have that confirmed of course. Well done." She turned to look at the detective. "What do you think, Jeff?"

"That was pretty impressive, Charles." He nodded solemnly. "You should be a detective."

"No thanks. So what happens now?"

"I still have a ton of work to do. I'm going to be up most of the night. You look like shit. You should get some sleep." The Chief led him back downstairs and into the fresh night air.

"Thanks...I think." Charles was immediately aware of the smell of the ocean. "I am going to bed right this minute- right over there!" He motioned across the street to the Edgartown Inn. "Oh! Before I forget, there's a bullet in that pillow."

Laurie looked at Charles in disbelief. "You're incredible." Of course, her team would have found the bullet as soon as they went over the scene with the proper equipment but the fact that Charles could go over everything in such a brief period of time with just his eyes and glean as much as he did was fascinating. "Tomorrow morning, I'm heading up to Menemsha. You still want to come?"

"I would actually. I'd be very interested to talk to a fisherman about a Great White Shark. It will be fascinating. Are you planning to talk to Karl Bass's family tomorrow?"

"I am. I might not be moving as quickly as I would like to be. It will depend on how much sleep I get."

"I'll get ready to go when I get up; I'm always up early. I'll have breakfast at the inn. They say they have the best breakfast in town. I'd like to see that for myself but I'll be ready by the time you get here. Text me when you are on your way."

"I'll do that." The Chief started back up to The Court House as Charles crossed the narrow street to his inn. She turned around again. "It was pretty great to have you around today. You helped... and I really enjoyed your company." She spoke with that awkwardness that comes when honest feelings are expressed between two adults.

"Thanks. I really enjoyed it too. Good night, Laurie." Charles walked up the stairs and into the Edgartown Inn. The lights were on in the main hall but it was quiet. Standing in front of his guestroom door, he could see through the kitchen to the back garden. The garden lights were illuminating the path to the guestrooms in the garden house but there was no movement. The dew glistened on the lawn, untouched. You never got this kind of quiet in downtown Toronto, he thought. Charles fished his room key out of a back pocket of his shorts, opened the door, walked in, and closed the door behind him. He stripped off, and climbed into bed. A shark attack, JAWSfest, and a murder- his mind should be reeling! He should be running on pure adrenaline. He fell asleep immediately.

12

The morning sun beamed in through gauzy, white lace curtains. Charles got out of bed and walked over to the dresser where his phone was charging; it was seven o'clock, still early by most people's standard but late for Charles. The morning was by far the best part of the day and the fact that so many wasted it was beyond him. The world was so happy first thing in the morning if you looked at it properly. He looked out the window. Joggers ran by and a few recreational sailors were making their way toward the harbour. Some people were walking back to their vacation homes with a newspaper under their arm and a coffee in their hand. Morning people were the best sort of people. If you walked down the street in the early morning in downtown Toronto, people still greeted each other with eye contact and a "Good morning!" The day in the big city wasn't hectic yet. Business and commerce hadn't sunk their fangs in and sucked out all of the humanity. The civility of an era gone past still existed in the early morning. Charles loved it. That humanity existed all day on Martha's Vineyard. That was part of its magic. He looked down the sun-gilded road outside his window. The sun was low and bright and there was no traffic yet on North Water. An early morning was an elegant way to start the day. Charles got dressed, grabbed the novel that he was reading, and walked out into the inn. He made sure that his room key was in his pocket before he closed the door. There was a lot of life back in the kitchen but the rest of the inn was still very quiet. There was a sign at the entrance to the dining room that read, "Please Wait To Be Seated". He stood by the sign. He couldn't see her but he could hear Edie's familiar voice chatting and laughing with her staff. After a couple of minutes she casually strode out of the kitchen with a large coffee mug in her hand. When she saw Charles she jerked into a less casual stance and strode toward him; she was surprised to see him standing there.

"Oh! You're an early riser!" She hurried over to him. "The dining room actually doesn't open until eight o'clock but there's coffee ready if you'd like a mug while you're waiting."

"That would be great. Am I allowed to drink it on the front porch? Would that be all right?"

"Oh absolutely! Absolutely! If I could, that's where I'd be drinking it." She laughed as she talked. "It's so beautiful at this time of day. People don't know what they're missing, do they?" Edie wore a black dress very similar to the one that she wore the day before. Charles got the feeling that she was one of those women who wore black far too often. Charles always thought that was sad; colour was so becoming on a pretty woman. Black was for Italian widows.

"No ma'am."

"Please, call me Edie. How do you take your coffee?" She reached up and grabbed a rather large ceramic mug that had been painted like the American flag. The mug didn't fit in her small hand.

"With milk, please, Edie." Charles watched and before he could say anything, she had poured in what would have been about a triple-milk. "Oh! Whoa! Just enough milk to change the colour! Sorry, I should have specified."

She poured a little coffee out and refilled with black coffee. "No problem. I'll have it down-pat before you leave." Passing him the coffee, she looked up and smiled. "I'll come out and get you when it's time for breakfast."

"Thank you very much. That's great." Charles turned and walked out on to the porch. Selecting the chaise closest to the door, he sat down. He didn't pick up his book right away but rather sat and absorbed his surroundings. This was how days were supposed to start. He sipped his coffee- delicious, strong and hot. Full trees in high season poured the early breakfast sun in golden rushes of honey and cream across North Water Street. There was a mild breeze but there was no coolness in it. The air was warm and thick with the scent of the ocean. Charles took a mouthful of coffee. This is how people should live, he thought. Where had the world gone wrong? He looked across the street. Police tape was stretched in front of The Court House in bright yellow reminder of last night's grisly scene. It was such a beautiful building, a century home in the Edgartown tradition of wooden shingle and black shutters. It was encased in a wrap-around porch dotted with cosy wicker furniture not unlike what Charles was sitting on now. It seemed so sad that such a warm and inviting building had such a terrible tragedy befall it. Window boxes lovingly planted with the ever-present red geraniums stretched up to the sun. They lived with a life that was blindly unaware of last night's goings on. It was all so much for Charles to wrap his head around. One moment you're here and one moment, you're not. Life marched on regardless. It doesn't matter who you are, the world stops for no one, he mused grimly. Charles sat, drank his coffee, and thought of Sean Burroughs, Mike Burroughs, and Karl Bass. There was a lot to sort out today. Charles looked at his iPhone; it was only 7:30. He finished his coffee and went inside. He had just enough time for a quick swim before breakfast.

*   *   *

The walk up North Water Street to the Fuller Street Beach was Edgartown at its finest. Pristine white captain's houses, each decorated with flowers and shrubs walled the narrow street. It was impossible not to make note of the perfume of a dozen rose bushes in the heavy sea air. Charles walked on the right hand side of the street, the side closest to the water. He tried to sneak a peek into the backyard of each house as he passed getting a glimpse of the harbour. Up ahead, the Edgartown Lighthouse guided him on, assuring him that he was heading in the right direction. Charles had never swum on this beach before but he had seen plenty of videos of it; it looked golden and perfect.

Across the street the horizon was dominated by The Harbor View Hotel. It was huge, majestic, and historic. It was sandy with white trim. Charles remembered reading about its construction. It was not long after the civil war, when the Vineyard was switching industries from the whaling industry to the tourist trade. The Harbor View had been built as an exclusive institution for fine travel and had rather successfully maintained this reputation. Charles was impressed with its opulence; however, when it all came down to it, Charles was more of an Edgartown Inn kind of guy. Immediately across from the hotel was a path that led down through the tall grass to the lighthouse and the beach. He weaved his way down the hill through grass and shrubbery that was taller than he was. When he came out on the other side he was on the beach. He walked toward the lighthouse and took a hard left, away from the harbour, and the ocean opened up in front of him. The beach was golden and soft and long. Charles looked into the distance but could not find the end of it. It went on for miles. There were two women sitting on towels, deep in conversation and one woman flying a kite with two little kids but other than that, the beach was his. Finding a spot away from the others, Charles threw down his sandals and towel, and then took off his T-shirt. He waded in to the water.

There was no shock of cold. There was no 'adjustment period'. The water was warm and inviting. Charles waded out until he was at upper-thigh and then pushed forward into a breaststroke, letting the water rush in around him. There is no other feeling in the world like swimming in the ocean. He dunked his head briefly and came back up- just enough to get wet. He swam out a little further. Charles remembered that there had been a shark attack in the vicinity and that this whole exercise might be a testament of stupidity but he thought the odds were in his favour. Scientists went out hunting sharks for weeks, filled the water with fish oil and blood, and they would sit and wait for days sometimes never seeing one. What was it they said? You were thirty times more likely to be struck by lightning? As far as he knew, Charles had never met anyone who had been struck by lightning although in some cases, it would certainly have explained a few things. He swam out about another thirty feet further from the beach and then turned parallel to the shore. Shark... the word had a stronger effect on the human nervous system than any other word in the English language. It caused more stress than 'fire' or 'rape'. The idea of being eaten alive by another animal while completely out of their element was the most terrifying thing that most people could imagine. Swimming in water that was too deep for them to touch the bottom. Swimming in water where the visibility was no more than five or six feet. Five or six feet of visibility when you're about to be hit by a two ton fish at fifty miles an hour was not a lot of warning. The fear was understandable, thought Charles. He started to swim back to shore. He knew that his body was being unreasonable but his heartbeat had increased and his breath was a little quicker. Shark. Stop it, he thought, you're being ridiculous. It was too late, his imagination had gotten the better of him and he swam faster to the beach. A cone shaped nose smashing into his gullet from behind was all he could picture. He breathed deeply and when his feet found the ocean floor, he stood. The water was waist deep. Doing his best not to lose his balance, Charles rushed from the water. On the shore he stood and tried to catch his breath. As he walked toward his towel and clothes Charles felt like the biggest idiot on the island. He laughed at himself. Towelling off, he turned and looked out over the water. Nothing. No fin, no screaming bathers in frothy eruptions of blood. Nothing. Charles remembered the bite radius on the remains of Karl Bass. Maybe it hadn't been such a good idea to go swimming after all. Maybe the risk hadn't been worth it. Something had done that to poor Karl. Great Whites had certainly been spotted in the area but they weren't swallowing bathers on a regular basis. Laurie had told him so yesterday but it wasn't anything that he didn't already know. Every shark sighting near a public beach got reported with remarkable speed on the JAWS Facebook page. The FINatics were all over that shit. If someone had been attacked on the beaches of Martha's Vineyard, it would go down as news story of the year. People would be creating paintings and sculptures depicting the attack for decades to come- a little gruesome but true. Charles walked down the beach back toward the lighthouse. When he passed the two women on towels they looked up at him and said, "Good morning!" He responded, in like. He loved morning people.

By the time he got to the Edgartown Inn, it was just after eight o'clock. He walked straight through the heavily decorated front hall and went into the dining room. He was quite hungry.

"How was your swim?" Edie welcomed him with her biggest smile to-date.

"Exhilarating." Charles replied blushing lightly at the thought of his embarrassing panic attack.

"Fabulous. Do you want to eat inside or outside? You strike me as an outside kind of guy."

"You have me pegged Edie."

"I thought so. This way." Edie led him through the garden to a small table for two. It was a beautiful place to eat breakfast.

The garden of the Edgartown Inn was wedged between the inn proper and the garden house. The buildings matched in their shingles and white trim and a lot of effort had been put into the garden itself. The tables sat on an interlocking red brick patio that was surrounded on all sides by mounds of neatly trimmed grass and shrubs. All of the shrubs offered red and pink flowers. Charles wished that he knew more about gardening but his interest in the subject was only recent and his knowledge was moderate at best. His mother would ask him what flowers there had been on his trip and he would not be able to tell her. He hated that. It didn't matter what the subject, he just hated not knowing. He made a mental note to ask Edie later. A traditional stone birdbath with a cherub pouring an urn was almost lost in the corner under vines of morning glories. A long white wooden staircase led up to the second storey of the garden house and the entire garden sat in the partial shade of an enormous oak tree. Charles thought that it might be nice to stay in the garden house for his next visit. He liked the thought of being in a separate building; however, he really liked the fact that his current room was so close to the front porch. It was such a pretty place. A young, slim, blonde girl came over to his table and set a piece of coffee cake in front of him.

"Would you like freshly squeezed juice or stewed prunes?" She smiled.

Charles did his best to conceal his horror. "Juice, please."

His waitress skipped off. *Stewed prunes?* Good god! He'd rather eat dirt! He had rarely heard of such an awful idea. Charles focused on the coffee cake that she had set in front of him. It was obviously homemade. The minute he sank his teeth into the cake, he forgot all about the prunes. It was still warm, fresh out of the oven- cinnamon, brown sugar, and butter, all swirling around in his mouth. The crumble topping fell in delicious nibbles on to his plate and he used his fingers to mop up every morsel. He would have licked the plate if he could be certain no one would see him. Edie said that they had been called the best breakfast in Edgartown and as far as he was concerned, they were off to a good start. His waitress returned with his juice and he told her that he would be having the full breakfast with bacon. She turned to leave but before she could, he stopped her. "Can I ask you something?"

"Sure!"

"Does anyone actually order the stewed prunes?" It was hard for him to say it without grimacing.

"All the time! I'd say that it was almost fifty-fifty."

"*Really?*" It was impossible for him to hide his surprise.

"They're better than they sound." She bounced off.

"They almost have to be." Charles said but she was gone. It wasn't long before his bacon and over-easy eggs came to the table. They were perfectly cooked but what made them spectacular was the side of toast. Every day the Edgartown Inn baked its own bread. They always had white bread but the other option changed daily. Today it was cheese bread. Thickly sliced, warm, cheese bread. This breakfast was spectacular. It was like having breakfast at your grandmother's, thought Charles. He decided then and there to eat-in every breakfast for the rest of his stay. He was just sopping up the rest of his yolk with cheese bread when Edie came hurrying over to his table. He thought for sure she would topple over on her high mules but she manoeuvred them expertly.

"Charles! Did you see this?" She slapped the newspaper down on the table in front of him and he stared at the headline in awe:

'SHARK VICTIM FOUND AT JAWS BRIDGE'

Commerce had won over good taste. Laurie would not be happy about this, nor would the rest of the island. This could affect tourism. That wouldn't bode well with anyone. He had to play dumb. "Oh Edie! That's terrible! Do they know who he was?"

"Nope. They say that he was an off-islander. That won't be good for my business I tell you. Not good at all." Edie furrowed her brow as she stared at the paper. She refilled Charles' coffee out of reflex and then looked at him with great consternation. "I don't want you going swimming anymore! Do you understand me? Not until they catch this thing..." She put a motherly hand on his shoulder.

"Edie, it's probably long gone by now. Besides, that body could have washed in from miles away."

"I suppose. I still don't want you swimming until the police learn more- promise me!"

"I promise." He smiled at her. It was nice that she was so concerned. His phone vibrated. He picked it up and read the screen. It read, "I'll be there in five." It was Laurie. "Edie I have to go. May I take this with me?"

"Oh sure, honey. I have a few."

He got up, folded the newspaper under his arm, and started to walk away but turned back. "Edie?" she looked up from tidying his table for the next guest. "That was *definitely* the best breakfast on the island. Save me a spot for tomorrow!" He left her beaming with pride.

13

"So, you've seen this then." Charles got into the waiting police cruiser with the newspaper in his hand but saw another copy lying between the front seats.

"Yes, it was inevitable. I brought it in case you hadn't read it yet." Laurie took one hand off of the steering wheel and reached for her coffee. She took the long luxurious gulp of someone who hadn't had much sleep.

"I haven't read it actually. Should I?" Charles stretched the seatbelt across his navy blue polo shirt and buckled himself in.

"It's not going to tell you anything new but you might want to read it so that *you* know what *they* know. You don't want to tell them anything new."

"I didn't think of that. Good call." Charles started reading the front-page article. There were two big accompanying photographs- one was the JAWS

Bridge and State Beach and the other was the classic JAWS poster, just to make sure that they were driving the fear home. It would certainly get the attention of all of the FINatics. Charles read the article. For all of the sensational journalist rhetoric, essentially it said what Edie had told him; a young boy had found a shark attack victim at State Beach, it didn't seem to be an islander. Police could not confirm identity.

"Okay. Where are we going now?" Charles looked down at the cup holders between the front seats. There was a second coffee. "Is this one mine?"

"If you want it, it is. If not, I'll drink it."

Charles picked up the cup.

"We are headed to the Bass family home."

"Where is that?" Charles took some coffee and decided that combined with all of the coffee he had at breakfast and before, he may have had his fill; Laurie might have to finish this one too.

"Well, technically it's in Edgartown but it's way up on the Edgartown West Tisbury Road. It's in the middle of nowhere really. There's nothing out there but bush."

Charles looked out the window in silence. He loved going for drives in the woods. He always had. Laurie had been right. Once they got out of the town proper, there was nothing to see but trees. There were drives and turn-offs from the main road but few of them were marked. Charles wondered how anyone made their way around parts of this island. It was easy to see why so many celebrities came here for vacation.

The entire island was beautiful but it could also be a great place to be if you didn't want to be found. Occasionally the side of the road was peppered by a row of mailboxes on wooden posts that didn't seem to co-ordinate with anything or anyone. He was finding this set up more and more curious. Charles figured that if he lived out here, he wouldn't even be able to find his own way home let alone anyone else finding him. He couldn't tell one drive from another and this was under a bright morning sun! Imagine what it must be like in the middle of the night. Split rail fences ran along the road as if guiding the cruiser in the right direction. They were Charles' favourite kind of fence, so organic. Especially these ones, they looked like they had been there for a hundred years...they probably had been. Laurie slowed the car and turned left onto a dirt road. It was impossible to tell whether or not it was a public road or a private drive. Some of the turn-offs were marked with small yellow signs stating that they were private but they were few and far between. Most of them were anybody's guess. The police cruiser crawled along until Charles could see a house in the woods. They pulled up in front and Laurie stopped the car. "You wait here." She said and Charles didn't argue.

The house was not ostentatious by any means but it was very nice just the same. It was a small single family home built of cedar planks greyed by the weather. It was not a new home. Charles guessed that it had been built about fifty years ago. There was a small porch leading up to the front door and an American flag waving proudly above it. The sun was just high enough to reach in over the trees and hit the flag when it flickered; it was an impressive sight. Charles wished that Canadians waved as many flags as Americans did. It was good to have that much pride in your country. The sloped roof was shingled and there were bushes planted under each white trimmed window. The windows were dark and there were no signs of life. Charles imagined that in a place like this, when the police rolled up, people usually came out to meet them at the door. He watched as Laurie opened the screen door and knocked. There was no response. Charles got out of the car. "I don't think there's anybody home."

"Me either." Laurie walked down the stairs. "I'm going to walk around in case they're out back. I doubt it though. It doesn't look like anyone has been here for a while." She walked around the far side of the house. When she turned the corner, she was out of sight. Charles began to look around. Native island birds chirped high above his head like happy children; the rustling trees egged them on. He started to walk around the small house. Why not meet the Chief around back? Along side the house there was a set of deep tire tracks. In some places still damp. The weather had been hot and dry. Even under this tree coverage, it wouldn't take too long for tire tracks to dry up and they had in some places but in others... Charles followed the tracks out back and came to a box truck with a trailer of about 25 feet. The Chief was standing beside it. "This hasn't been here that long." Charles said to the Chief. "The tracks are still pretty fresh in some spots."

"I thought I asked you to stay in the car?" Laurie lifted an eyebrow and grinned.

"Oh. Well, there's nobody here."

"Yeah, that's true." Laurie looked up at the huge white box truck.

"Do you recognise this truck?"

"Nope. It has California plates." Laurie walked up and down the length of the truck. "There aren't enough of these on the island for it to go unnoticed."

"Want me to take down the license plates?" Charles got out his iPhone.

"Already did. Who ever drove this truck brought it here directly and hasn't moved it since. One of my officers would have seen it."

"The steamship authority would have record of it coming over, no?"

"Yes. That's probably worth looking into." Laurie's cell phone rang and she pulled it out of her pocket and answered it. "Are you kidding me? They're two days early! I'll be right there." She hung up quickly and hurried toward the car. "We have to go! Now!"

"What's happened?" Charles ran to the car. Laurie had already started the ignition.

"Karl Bass's autopsy report just came in!"

*   *   *

The Chief walked in to her office with Charles in tow and found a sealed envelope on her desk. She picked it up and tore it open as she sat down in her black leather chair. Charles sat down across from her. They sat in silence while the Chief read. When she was done, she passed it to Charles. She said nothing.

Charles picked up the report and started reading. Much of it was to be expected. There were several notes outlining the wounds from the shark and missing limbs and sections of the sternum. On the report there were two basic outlines of a human body, one front and one rear view. Both had been marked indicating what pieces had been removed and where. There was also a black dot toward the lower spine drawn in by the coroner. Charles looked for the notes that accompanied that mark. It was right there under 'Probable Cause of Death'. It read, 'Gunshot'.

"Gunshot!" He looked at the Chief in disbelief.

"So it would seem. They pulled a bullet out of his spine, forty calibre."

"Is that significant?"

"It was certainly significant to Karl Bass. It's also significant to us because it's the same calibre bullet that we pulled out of Sean Burroughs' pillow last night." The Chief looked as grim as Charles had ever seen her look.

"I don't believe in coincidences."

"I'm starting to think that I don't either."

Charles continued reading. "It says that they found a piece of pitch pine lodged in his ocular socket." He kept reading. "Also, he had bits of scrub oak under his fingernails." There was still more. "They found traces of pogy oil, ground cat food, and cornmeal in the creases of his skin."

"Almost sounds like he was tossed in a dumpster. That's a helluva combination. Don't you think? He must have smelled pretty sweet. Does it mean anything to you?"

"Not the pitch pine and scrub oak, I've never heard of either one," said Charles.

"I have. The island is lousy with both of them. If he died on land then I have a pretty good idea of where to start looking. The other crap means nothing to me...yet."

"That combination is a pretty popular recipe for homemade chum." Charles had the Chief's full attention and he nodded his head in reassurance. "It's true. I mean if you were a regular fisherman, you would have rotten fish bits leftover that would make a much tastier chum but if you weren't a fisherman that would be one way to make it. It's a popular method used by mainlanders because it's cheap."

"What the hell is pogy oil?" The Chief looked disgusted. She may not know what it was but she did know that it was unpleasant.

"Well, it's fish oil. You know, from a pogy which is a common forage fish."

"What on earth for?" The Chief stared at him.

130

"To attract a shark. A forage fish is a fish that is a main food source for larger marine life- seals, whales, and definitely sharks." Charles stated. "It all makes sense now. Karl was murdered on land and then the body was dumped in the ocean and the water chummed to get rid of the evidence. It almost worked too. Creative man, our murderer."

"We need to confirm that those bullets were from the same gun but in the meantime, I'm going to work under the assumption that they are. It would be pretty incredible if they weren't. Besides, I don't want to think about the implications if they're not!" Laurie looked at her watch. "Oh shit! We need to get up to the hospital and talk to Mike Burroughs, then get to Menemsha, and then we'll grab some lunch."

"Alright. As long as we aren't having apple fritters in the squad car for lunch. I'm all frittered out."

"Deal."

*   *   *

Charles and the Chief drove the now familiar route to the Martha's Vineyard Hospital. After they parked the car, they walked in through the same emergency entrance that they had used when they came to see Casey, the boy who had discovered Karl in the water. The same nurse, Connie, was on duty and she greeted them with the same exuberance that she had displayed on their previous visit. It was a good quality to have in a job like hers. Charles imagined that most people would be easily mired down in the tragedy that was part and parcel to being an emergency room nurse. Somehow Connie remained buoyant.

"Good morning Chief! Good morning Mr Williams!" She smiled a genuine smile at them.

"How do you know Mr Williams, Connie?" The Chief grinned a half-smile at Connie.

"It's a small island, Chief. You ought to know that better than anyone. You'll be here after that nice Mr Burroughs. He's in the same room that the young boy was in the last time you were here. He was sleeping the last time that the nurse checked in on him."

"Thanks Connie." The Chief walked past the desk and turned to go down the hallway toward Mike's room but she paused and turned back toward Charles. "Why don't you come with me? I think that it might actually do this guy some good to have a friendly face in the room. Someone he knows. He seems pretty high strung."

"He is at that."

They walked down the short hallway to the door that Charles had seen the Chief knock on when they had been here to see Casey. She knocked again with the same quick three knocks and entered without waiting for a response.

Mike was lying in bed with the covers pulled up to his armpits but he wasn't asleep. The life that had emitted from his eyes non-stop, his boundless energy was gone. His fresh pink colour had been replaced with stale grey pallor. He lay on his back with the head of the adjustable bed at a forty-five degree angle. He stared out of the window with no expression. There was no acknowledgement that they had entered the room. Charles and the Chief stood at the foot of the bed for a couple of minutes waiting for him to turn and look at them. He didn't. The Chief spoke first.

"Mr Burroughs?"

Nothing.

Charles decided to give it a go. "Mike? Mike, it's Charles, buddy." It took a few seconds but Mike started to turn his head. He looked at Charles and smiled slightly.

"Charles? Hi. What brings you down here?" Mike spoke softly and his voice was hoarse. No doubt his throat was raw from the night before.

"We're here to talk about your brother, Mr Burroughs." The Chief was speaking in the same soft voice that she had used last night at The Kelley House.

Mike turned his head slightly to look at the Chief. "I'm sorry officer but my brother is dead."

"We need to ask you a couple of questions about that. Can you answer a couple of questions Mr Burroughs?"

"Yes. He died yesterday at the hotel. There was so much blood...so much blood." Mike turned back toward the window. His face was expressionless.

"Mr Burroughs, did you see anyone at your hotel room yesterday? A woman perhaps?"

Nothing.

"Mike?" Charles asked again. "Mike, did Sean have any friends on the island? Did he see a girl yesterday?"

Nothing.

The Chief looked at Charles and motioned toward the door. It was time to go. "Okay, Mike. We're going to go but we'll come back and talk some more soon. You get some rest." They turned to go.

"Charles?" Mike spoke as they hit the door.

The Chief and Charles turned around at the sound of Mike's voice. It was so soft that it was almost inaudible.

Mike showed no expression and continued to stare out the window. "I made him come to the island." Tears ran out of the outer corners of his eyes, down past his ear, and dripped on to the pillow. He made no effort to wipe them away. "He didn't want to come at all."

14

The drive through Chilmark to Menemsha was silent. Mike Burroughs was dealing with some pretty heavy emotions and could be of no use to their investigation in his current state. Charles was not so much worried whether or not Mike would be of use to them but rather whether or not he would ever be of use to himself again. He had lost his only sibling, a twin. That must be akin to losing half of your soul. To have the guilt of being responsible for that death attached to that tragedy was unfathomable to Charles. Of course, Mike was not responsible for his brother's death any more than Charles was or the organiser of JAWSfest for that matter. The only person responsible was the person who had pulled the trigger. There was no excuse for taking the life of another human being. The world had to exist on that principle or civilisation didn't work. Now, there were two victims from two bullets likely from the same gun and in as many days. That was probably some sort of new ghoulish record on the Vineyard. This was why Laurie had left Boston. She had likely been looking forward to a long career of pot-smoking high school kids, beer brawls, and traffic violations. Double homicide was a bit more than the Vineyard could take. Two people in his JAWS group murdered by the same gun on the same island within forty-eight hours. Charles didn't believe in coincidences. Each one was really a question to be answered. So what were the two questions? Which two people had been murdered? Karl Bass and Sean Burroughs. How were they murdered? They were shot with a .40 Glock more than likely. It was a popular gun. Even most of the Police Force carried the .40 Glock. Whose gun shot them? They didn't know yet. Why were they shot? They didn't know yet. Charles knew that he had the answers in his head; he just had to find them.

Menemsha was a fishing village, first and foremost. Fishing families had been there for generation after generation. While the harbours of Oak Bluffs, Edgartown, and Vineyard Haven were populated with luxury cruisers and sailboats, Menemsha harbour was filled with draggers and lobster boats, some as big as forty feet. Small weathered shacks, rusted workboats, dinghies, and fishing equipment of every kind littered the harbour in bright colours. A row of whitewashed cedar homes sat on a steep hillside keeping it all under watchful protection. Charles imagined that the homes belonged to the fisherman but you never know. The houses were immaculately maintained and had a beautiful view of the harbour, the beach, and the ocean; they had probably been sold off to New York lawyers for a pretty penny a long time ago. Laurie pulled the car up to the southeast corner of the harbour basin and looked down the water. She looked at her watch. "His boat's not here; let's have lunch first." She turned the car around and headed back up to Basin Road. They turned left and drove down to the harbour mouth and parked.

"Here?" Charles looked around. It wasn't exactly downtown Edgartown.

"No place better on the island, I promise you." She got out of the car and shut the door. Charles got out too. He followed her to a picnic table in front of Larsen's Fish Market. "Wait here. What do you want to drink?"

"Just water will be fine. How about what I'd like to eat?"

"Trust me." Laurie disappeared into the building. There were people sitting at picnic tables on the sand all around him busy with their own lunches. He tried to see what they were eating but couldn't quite make it out without being obvious. Charles had to admit it was a beautiful place to eat lunch, right on the beach, completely informal. The salty sea air was warm and thick. There was a pleasant wind. It was another perfect day on the Vineyard. It was the perfect cover for the horrifying events that had taken place of late. No one would ever guess that anything could go wrong here. Laurie came back ten minutes later with her arms piled high. She set down the food and pulled two bottles of water out of her windbreaker pocket.

"What do we have here?" Charles was a lot hungrier than he had realised.

Laurie placed some trays in front of him. "We have steamed mussels, oysters on the half-shell, and the best god-damned lobster rolls on the eastern seaboard!"

"Fantastic!" Charles' mouth was watering. "I have been looking for the best lobster roll on the island since I got here! No menu has struck me quite right. This place could do it."

"Damn right it does. You're never going to find fresher seafood than this. It all just came out of that harbour right there." She motioned over her shoulder as she sucked a mussel out of its shell. "Dig in!"

They ate in silence listening to the rolling waves on Menemsha Beach.

After eating the best lunch that Charles could ever remember having, they got back in the car and drove around to the basin of the Menemsha Harbour. Laurie saw something that made her happy because she hurried out of her seat belt and said one word, "Great!"

They walked down a muddy path along the harbour until they came to a grey shack that looked like it could very well have been the first building constructed on the island. The roof was sloped and some of the shingles missing. The windows were opaque at best with dirt. By dramatic contrast, the tackle that leaned against the shack was clean and sparkling in the sun- well used but well maintained. There was no one to be seen but there was a small trawler tied to the dock.

"Keith!" Laurie stepped down onto the dock and walked out. Charles stayed back. "Keith!" She repeated.

A voice shouted out from inside the boat. "That you Chief?"

"It is! Permission to come aboard Captain Hurtubise, sir?"

"Permission granted!" A stout man with snow-white hair appeared from below decks. He had a small white moustache and a trim white beard. To Charles, he looked like Colonel Saunders from Kentucky Fried Chicken. "Laurie it's good to see you, chere!" He gave her a big hug and kissed her on the cheek. He had an accent of some sort. It might have even been French Canadian muddled in with New England. Captain Hurtubise looked down from the boat and motioned toward Charles. "Who's this young fella?"

"Keith, this is one of my oldest and dearest friends, Charles Williams. Charles, this is Captain Hurtubise."

Charles raised his voice to be heard from where he stood. "Pleasure to meet you sir!"

"Well, we'll see about that lad." The captain turned back to Laurie. "I thought that I was your oldest friend?" He grinned.

"You're my oldest anything!" They both laughed. Charles tried to figure out just how old the captain was. He could have been fifty or eighty and anything in between. Laurie turned to Charles. "I met Keith and his wife at church when I first came to the island. They took pity on me not having any family and started inviting me over for Sunday supper."

"So, what can I do for ya?" the captain went about the business at hand, cleaning some indeterminate machine parts that he had hauled up with him from below deck.

"Well, if you've read the papers today, you must have seen the story about the shark attack on the off-islander."

"I did. Read it over my breakfast on the boat. Missus wrapped it up with my food today. She's good for that. Takes care of me pretty good. When are you going to find someone for you to take care of like that? You're not getting any younger mon petit chou!"

"Yes, I know Keith, you say that every time. Can we try to keep on track please?"

"Sure. Sure. Continue. Just sayin' is all. You know, you really should come up for supper. The Catherine is always askin' after ya."

Laurie shook her head. "I will Keith. I promise. Now this guy was attacked by a Great White. I was wondering if you had any shark trouble recently or if you or anyone else down here has caught one, maybe? Any signs that there might be one around."

"Well, I'd say that a half-eaten man on State Beach was a pretty good indication, mon petit chou. Wouldn't you?"

"Yes but we think that he might have had some help. He was covered in- what was he covered in again Charles?" Laurie looked down off the boat at Charles who stepped a little closer to be heard a little better.

"There were traces of pogy oil, cat food, and cornmeal in the creases of his epidermis."

"Where?" The captain scrunched up his face like he had just been yelled at in a foreign tongue.

"On his skin. It was all over his skin." Laurie interjected.

"Well, why didn't you say that, man? You're boyfriend here fancies himself a bit of a smarty-pants, does he? Jesus H. Christ." Captain Keith Hurtubise shook his head. "Well, that's mainlander's chum. That's what that is. Your friend was used for fish food. Someone friggin' baited him to make sure of it. Nasty bit o' business that is. Don't go thinking that it was anyone around here either!" He waved a finger around the harbour. "These boys would rather hang for murder than be discovered using some piss-poor chum substitute like that to attract a porker! Your killer is from America. I'll tell ya that for free."

"So, no sign of a white shark?" Laurie asked.

"Can't see it. One of the boys here would have said something. Fish would be scarce or someone would have caught it by now. You don't keep catchin' a porker a secret- not on this island. It would have ended up in the paper! Now say you'll come for supper. You can bring smarty-pants if you like."

Laurie laughed and patted the man kindly on the head. "Alright. This Sunday, I'll come over for an early supper. Tell Catherine to let me know if it's a problem."

"Oh she'll be tickled pink! She'll make up a roast with all the fixin's! Yorkshire puddings an' all." The captain helped Laurie down off the boat and turned toward Charles. "You come too smarty-pants!"

"Thank you very much sir but I'll be back on the mainland by then." Charles waved.

"What in god's name would you want to go back there for?" The captain shook his head in disgust. "Well, if you change your mind, the offer's open."

Charles and Laurie walked back to the car and got in. She started the ignition.

"So..." started Charles. "No shark?"

"No shark," said Laurie and she drove back to Edgartown.

15

Back at The Whaling Church, JAWSfest was proceeding swimmingly. The banner with 'JAWSfest: The Tribute 2012' written in big red, blue, and gold letters swayed majestically across the pillars of the church. In front of the church steps was the same makeshift reception desk that had been there the day before. Volunteers were still selling tickets, handing out wristbands, and answering questions of every kind. One of the ladies was Rebecca Thompson who had introduced the film at Owen Park in Vineyard Haven. Charles approached her. When he got close, she looked up at him. Her eyes were red and a bit puffy. She must have seen his reaction and offered an explanation up front.

"Allergies! They're simply awful," she said.

"Oh, I'm sorry to hear that. Mine have been all right. Whatever I'm allergic to must not be on the island."

"You're lucky." She wiped the bottom of her nose with an embroidered hanky she was holding in her left hand. She was a well-put together woman. She wore expensive clothes that looked as if they were from boutiques off-island. She was probably only here for the season, thought Charles. While she was definitely American, her style had a slightly European bent to it. Her hair was swept up and her perfume was strong. She looked directly at Charles, squared her shoulders, and forced a smile. "Now, what can I do for you?"

"I'm looking for a friend of mine. I was wondering if you could tell me if he has checked in and at what time?" Charles smiled ingratiatingly.

"I might be able to help. What's his name?"

"Karl Bass."

"Oh, Mr Bass. I don't believe he has checked in actually. I will double check." Rebecca picked up her list and started through it. "No. I'm sorry but he still hasn't checked in. Strange too. He's the only V.I.P. bracelet left. He paid his three hundred dollars; you'd think that he would show up."

"Do you know Karl?" Charles asked.

"No. I've never met the man. It's just that another man just asked about him this morning too. Maybe they have already connected."

"Who asked about him?" Charles pried.

"Tim Oakes- a handsome man, a big man. That's why I remember his name. I remember thinking, wow! You're as big as an Oak! Do you know him?"

"As a matter of fact, I do. Thank you Ms Thompson, you've been very helpful." Charles walked away thinking about Karl Bass. Well, that might explain why Karl was on the island, it was for JAWSfest after all. It also explained why there was nobody home at the Bass home; however, it did not explain why he was dead. Tim Oakes, eh? That's cool. Charles would like to meet him. He was the other feather in the JAWS group's cap. They had actually worked on the set of the movie. He wouldn't mind hearing a story or two firsthand. Larry and Brooke had mentioned congregating at the Newes From America Pub at The Kelley House. He decided to head down there; a pint would be very welcome. Besides, he was curious to know what the group had to say on the shark attack at the JAWS Bridge.

*   *   *

The Newes From America was a wonderful pub. Everything that Charles thought a public house should be. The walls were wood and brick and the floor was stone. All of the furniture was wooden and the ceilings were low. It was ell shaped and not very big so it always seemed cramped. Being inside felt like being in a British pub out on the moors about two hundred years ago. Charles loved it. The food was delicious too. Seeing as it wasn't a very big place, it didn't take long to see that his friends had taken over several tables toward the back. Motioning him over with a mouth full of chicken wings, Larry pulled out a chair for him.

"Bloody Hell! Where have you been mate? We've been waiting to talk to you all day!" He waved their waitress over and ordered a Guinness for Charles and one for himself.

"What for?" Charles sat back and smiled, happy not to be dealing with corpses and/or the bereaved for a little while at least.

"We've got a dead guy on State Beach, eaten by a shark, and you're hangin' with the local constabulary! What do you think we want to talk to you about?" He grabbed him playfully around the neck and shook him. "Now, what is going on? Who is it?"

"I'm sorry but all I know is what was in the paper this morning! They got that from us."

"*Us?* Will you listen to that! He's one of them!" Larry laughed. "You're pullin' me fuckin' leg. I know ye got more than that but you're playin' it tight lipped. Well, that's all right. Fair enough. You're probably not allowed to tell. Fair enough." Larry took a swig of his beer. "Well can you tell us this then- what the hell has happened to Mike and Sean? Nobody's heard from them since yesterday."

Charles' heart sank. Nobody knew. This was terrible. He had to tell them. They were Mike's friends- they had to know. They didn't know Sean very well, not many of them anyway, but they knew Mike. "Alright. I'm going to tell you something but you all have to keep this to yourselves; although, I'm sure that the story is being written as we speak and it will be in tomorrow's newspaper." The whole crew of them leaned in toward Mike, excited about getting the inside scoop from the Edgartown Police. "Sean is dead."

None of them moved. This was far from the juicy bit of island gossip that they had been hoping for. Not the story of the brothers fighting over Sean bringing several women back to the hotel room that they had been expecting. No, this was altogether different. One of their peers was gone and it hit them hard.

"What happened?" Brooke was the first to speak.

"Um...he was shot." Charles braced himself for their reaction.

"What!" There was a collective astonishment. The girls, Brooke, Jackie, and Tina, were more emotional and tears welled up in their eyes as much as they tried to fight it. The men were stoic.

"Please, try to keep it down." Charles tried to lower their voices.

"What happened? Where's Mike? Is he all right?" Jackie asked.

"Sean was shot in his bed in his hotel room. His brother discovered him not long after the movie yesterday night. Mike is not well. He has been admitted to the hospital but I don't think that he is seeing visitors at this point. We don't know why Sean was shot or by whom but Police Chief Knickles has asked me to assist in the investigation. I will certainly let you know more as I know more." He picked up his Guinness and savoured three gulps in a row. "It's been a stressful couple of days."

"I guess it has," said Larry. He put his hand on his friend's shoulder. "Is there anything that we can do to help?"

"Not at this point, no. I can't say that there is except keeping it quiet. As I said, I'm sure that it will end up in the paper any minute. As soon as Mike is seeing visitors, I'll let you know. I know it would do him the world of good to see some friends. He's a bit out of it right now."

"I can imagine. That must be just terrible. The poor darlin'!" Brooke wiped her face with the napkin that came with her chicken wings. She picked up her glass and raised it as high as she could. "To Sean and Mike!"

The group all raised a glass and crashed them together. "To Sean and Mike!" They all shouted in unison.

"So you figure that they're going to close the beaches after that fella being attacked?" Eddie asked. He had his arm around his wife Tina who was visibly shaken by the news of the Burroughs brothers.

"You know, I'm not sure. I don't know what the island protocol is. I don't think that they can actually close the beaches like they did in JAWS but they can put up signs that say 'Swim at Your Own Risk'. I remember seeing some in photographs from the Cape last summer. Anyway, the Chief and I went down to Menemsha to talk to a fisherman to see if any of them had seen any signs of a Great White in the vicinity of late. They hadn't. It might have been a fluke. Besides the tide could have washed him in from anywhere. The shark is probably long gone by now." Charles drank more Guinness.

"Well that's good...and a little disappointing, if you know what I mean." Eddie said.

"That's terrible Eddie!" Tina elbowed him in the stomach.

"I just meant that I liked sharks is all. I didn't want anyone to die or anything! Jeez!"

"Yeah, I know what you mean. I would like to have seen a Great White. Would have been cool..." Charles mused.

The frosted glass door of the pub let in a lot of light so when it was eclipsed, everyone turned to see who was coming in. There was a big tower of a man standing in the doorway looking across the pub at their table. He had wild blonde curly hair that had been bleached by the sun and the busted nose of a hockey player.

"Oakes!" Tim jumped up from the table and rushed over to greet him. The two Tims seemed to know each other quite well. There was a vigorous handshake and then they walked over to the table.

"Guys you know Tim Oakes, right? Tim do you know everyone here?"

"I think so." Oakes looked at Charles. "I don't think that we've met but I recognise you from Facebook. I'm Tim Oakes but please call me Oakes, everyone does."

"Oakes. I'm Charles." He held out his hand and Oakes shook it a lot harder than Charles thought was necessary.

"Good to meet you buddy." Oakes sat down where Tim had arranged a chair for him and they started talking. A few of them seemed really excited to see him. He had, after all, worked on the movie in person. "This fest is bullshit so far don't you think?"

"Actually, I think it's pretty cool. What don't you like about it?" Charles felt the energy of the room change.

"There's nobody here who has a fucking clue what's going on. It's the same old shit. It's poorly organised. The first JAWSfest- now, that was good. Benchley was still alive; Scheider was here. That was a fucking JAWSfest. This is crap." Oakes pounded the table with his left fist.

"That would have been awesome to see those guys. They were class acts." Charles was cut off.

"I'd be speaking at this one if those guys were around. They were close personal friends. I spoke at the first one. There was a lot going on. None of this 'Women of JAWS' shit. Who gives a fuck about that?"

"I actually thought that was very interesting. A bunch of us went to that. Those women were wonderful." Charles said and Tina nodded her agreement.

Larry spoke up, "I liked it. Quite good really."

"It was crap. Bunch of old broads going on about shit that nobody cares about." Oakes looked for the waitress. He wanted his beer.

"Oakes did you hear about the shark victim found at State Beach? Pretty crazy, eh?" Tim was trying to change the subject. It was obvious that he thought that Oakes was pretty cool. Charles did not.

"I did read that. It came as a bit of a surprise that's for sure- quite a coincidence. We didn't have any sharks bothering us when we were here in seventy-four. That's for sure. We spent so much time out in that ocean that it was on everyone's mind all the time. Especially with Bruce the shark looming there. It didn't matter whether he was working or not, that shark was a scary piece of work up close. That Joe Alves is a genius. He's a good friend. You know I helped design that shark? I did. Did I tell you that story?" Oakes' beer arrived and the group started asking him questions about the production. Charles lost interest. It was obvious that this guy was re-living his glory days. Charles wasn't going to hold it against him but he didn't want to listen to it either.

"I'm going to take off, guys. I'll see you again soon. It was good to finally meet you Oakes. We'll see each other around I'm sure." He held out his hand and Oakes shook it again- harder than necessary.

"I hope so. Take care buddy," said Oakes.

Charles almost puked. Buddy, right. He walked out of the Newes into the evening sun. It was bright. He pulled out his phone and called the Chief. "Hey what are you doing?"

"I'm just getting off duty. Why? What did you have in mind?" Laurie picked up her cell right away.

"Supper." Charles was hungry.

"Excellent. I'll come and pick you up. Where are you?"

"Can you get me at The Edgartown Inn?"

"Yes, I can. Twenty minutes." Laurie hung up.

16

The Chief lived on East Chop Drive in Oak Bluffs. The house was about a century old and on the water. There was a large jetty on her property but she didn't own a boat. It was not a large house by any means and it was sided in weathered grey shingles, of course, and the trim was white. Charles loved it. The combination of the rocky soil and the elements had made it difficult to grow most things but there were a few short trees that had been moulded into odd shapes by the strong sea winds that picked up at a moment's notice. There used to be a garage out front but the previous owners had converted it into a guesthouse. The Chief was between renters. Having a lodger was a good source of income in the summer. Almost all of the year-round residents had figured out a way to capitalise on the summer dinks. Income for a lot of the islanders could be scarce in the winter months. You had to make it when you could. When Laurie had told Charles that they were going to eat at her place he had been delighted. Not exactly a world traveller, Charles was looking forward to a home cooked meal. They had stopped at the Stop & Shop on Main Street in Edgartown and picked up steaks and potatoes for the barbeque and all the makings for a great salad. Laurie assured him that she had plenty of wine and a surprise for dessert, so he needn't worry about getting anything.

They entered Laurie's house and Charles fell in love. It was warm and inviting. The walls were done in a whitewashed pine and there were rag rugs on the floor. Most of the furniture was antique wood in mix-matched colours. Charles could tell that it had once been a series of smaller rooms like so many of the older homes on the island but modern renovations had knocked down walls and the living spaces had a much more open concept. From his position at the front door, Charles could see right through to the kitchen and the large picture windows showcasing the view of the ocean. He took his shoes off and walked through, flabbergasted. "This is beautiful, Laurie! This house must have set you back a fortune!"

"Well, it wasn't cheap but my husband had a pretty good insurance policy. I would not have been able to do this otherwise." Laurie smiled at her friend's frankness regarding money. She remembered that had been typical of Torontonians. Islanders would never bring up money so directly. They'd be dying to and

154

they would discuss it behind your back but they would never bring it up to your face. She pulled a bottle of red wine down from her wine rack and started to open it.

"Do you mind if I have white?" Charles asked. "I can't do red. It just doesn't agree with me anymore."

"No problem. I have the perfect solution." Laurie went into her stainless steel fridge and pulled out a bottle of white for Charles. "I have a Gewürztraminer! Are you familiar with it?"

"I am actually. The Gewürztraminer is the white wine that drinks like a red. It's perfect for red meats."

"I should have known. Jesus Christ." Laurie was going to grimace but decided to laugh instead.

"No! It's really cool actually. It's a German wine but the grape is originally French from a small town on the French/German border called Tramine hence 'traminer'. The French hated it; they claimed that it was too spicy for wine but the Germans, who like a stronger bodied wine, were quite fond of it. That's where the name comes from- 'gewürz' is 'spice' in German. 'Gewürztraminer'! Cool, eh?" Charles was beaming.

Laurie shook her head. "You're amazing. I mean you're a total nerd but you're amazing. I wish I knew half of the shit that you knew." She poured him a glass of wine. "Here, drink this. I'm going to go and get changed out of my uniform. I'll be right back." Laurie walked out of the kitchen and up the stairs to the second floor.

Charles went into the sunroom and sat on a wooden club chair with overstuffed burlap potato sack cushions. It was easy to see why islanders never wanted to go to the mainland or "America" as they called it. He sipped his wine and watched the surf roll in on the pebble beach. Laurie had a wonderful set up here. There was no reason to come out this far on East Chop unless you lived here. Charles thought that there might be some tourists that came out to see the East Chop Lighthouse but probably not too many. There were so many lighthouses to see on the Vineyard and this one was so far out. In the distance, Charles watched the Wood's Hole Ferry on its way to Oak Bluffs. The decks were full. No surprise really, it was Friday after all. There would be weekenders and vacationers and some islanders. Everyone wanted part of the magic of Martha's Vineyard. This was a place that was completely separate from the modern day world. The island bred happiness because of that fact. People walked around stress-free. Cell phone reception and Wi-Fi were notoriously bad on the island. It forced people into a certain level of disconnect. Even the basics were a little behind the times. There wasn't even a traffic light on the island. That's the way that everyone wanted it to be.

"There! That's better." Laurie came into the sunroom with her own glass of wine. She was dressed in a pair of chocolate brown yoga pants and a baby blue hooded sweatshirt with a chocolate embroidered flower on the chest. Her streaked blonde hair was back in a ponytail and her make-up had been washed off. Charles had forgotten how naturally feminine and pretty Laurie was. Her eyes sparkled with life and her smile was wide and genuine. She seemed to take on a different tone in her uniform. The uniform totally hid her figure for one. That was probably just as well. Dealing with drunks or rowdy teens would be a lot harder if they knew how attractive she was.

"Wow! You look great!" Charles remarked.

"You don't like the uniform?" Laurie lifted one eyebrow playfully.

"The uniform is very nice but it hardens you somehow. You look softer and younger in street clothes."

Laurie laughed, "I would hardly call these street clothes! These are my workout clothes! I won't be wearing these in the Stop & Shop any time soon."

"You know what I mean. Don't quibble."

"Who says 'quibble' besides you? That's what I'd like to know." She smiled to let her friend know that she was teasing him. She loved that he was smart and had a decent command of the English language. Sadly that was largely becoming a skill of the past. "Come into the kitchen and talk to me while I make supper."

"I'll help if you like." Charles got up and followed her into the kitchen.

It was a country kitchen to be sure but very modern- wooden cupboards with windows in the doors, stainless steel appliances, and wooden chopping blocks. The curtains were light and gauzy.

There was an island separating the kitchen from the living/dining room and Charles pulled out a stool from underneath it. Laurie brought him a bowl and a knife. She then went to the fridge and pulled out the vegetables that they had bought that afternoon. "Here, wash these and make a salad. You can make a salad, right?"

"I'm on it, Chief." Charles started with the Boston lettuce. He turned on the faucet attached to the island sink and started rinsing the lettuce. "Oh, I may have found our mystery woman."

"What mystery woman?" Laurie was cutting potatoes in half and slicing onions to wrap together in tinfoil for the barbeque.

"Sean's mystery woman."

"You *may* have found her? Would you care to elaborate on that for me?" Laurie turned around to look at him. The seriousness that went with the uniform had returned to her face.

"Well, it's not exactly enough to go on but when I went to the JAWSfest headquarters at the Whaling church this afternoon, this woman was working the information table and I'll swear on my life that she was wearing Lolita Lempicka. I don't think that she had it on right at that moment- it's very heavy for the daytime; however, it's really distinct and I would imagine very rare for this island. I've smelled a lot of Chanel on this island. Lolita Lempicka is a little out there for this crew. Anyway, it's the same scent from the pillow and the closet. It's all earthy woods and black liquorice."

"How are you so familiar with Lolita Lempicka?" Laurie stared at him incredulously.

"Well, I was reading this article..." Charles was cut off.

"Of course you were! Do you do anything but read?" Laurie threw her hands up in the air. "Unbelievable..."

Charles ignored her. "I was reading this article about Charlize Theron being the model picked for the Chanel no.5 ads and I wondered how popular Chanel no.5 really was these days. So I looked it up. Turns out it's very popular which I thought was very cool. Then I wondered what the top perfumes in the world were these days so I looked *those* up. I remember that Lolita Lempicka got a favourable mention as the most distinct perfume of 2012. The word 'distinct' made me curious. The next day on the way to work, I went into the store and smelled it. It is odd but not unpleasant. The article said that it went on very heavy but lightened to a beautiful scent. So I sprayed some on. It did get much better as time passed. I don't know how women decide in the store. Perfume really changes throughout the day." Charles chopped as he talked. When he was finished his story he looked up at Laurie who was quietly staring at him. "What?"

"You sprayed the perfume on in the store and wore it all day?" Laurie's smirk had returned.

"Yes. I wanted to see how it changed. The article was pretty clear." Charles was serious. He was quite used to people not understanding his thought processes; it didn't bother him.

"You're one of a kind, Charles. So you think this woman is our girl eh? We'd better talk to her. Would you know her if you saw her again. Can you give me a description?"

"Actually, now that I think about it, her eyes were all puffy and her nose was running. She said that it was her allergies but she could have been upset about something. Her name is Rebecca Thompson."

"Oh, I know her. She lives here from June through September and then flies around Europe." Laurie was wrapping her potatoes and putting them in a bowl. When she was done, she ran out to the back deck and quickly threw them on the grill.

Charles waited for her to return before talking. "I thought as much. Her style is very continental. She's a very attractive woman all in all."

"Yes, I'd agree with that. If I'm not mistaken, she's got a place just off of Edgartown West Tisbury Road. Actually, it's not that far from where Karl Bass's family home is... just the other side of Manuel F. Correllus. That's interesting." Laurie was off somewhere else, deep in thought.

"Who's Manuel F. Correllus and why is that interesting?"

"Well, I'll be damned. Something you don't know. Actually, I don't know who he was either. I'm assuming he was an islander who bought the land and donated it. Anyway, do you remember what they found on Karl Bass's corpse? How we knew he was murdered on land?"

"Yes. He had pitch pine in his ocular socket and scrub oak under his fingernails."

"Exactly. When I said that they meant something to me, I meant Manuel F. Correllus State Forest. It's lousy with the stuff. I think that we should go up to have a chat with Ms Thompson and maybe have a hike through the park. What do you think?"

"I'm in." Charles had finished chopping the vegetables and was layering them in the salad bowl. They smelled like summer- fresh, earthy, and delicious.

"Great. With all the goings on, you haven't told me much about JAWSfest. Are you enjoying it? A lot of work went into it. Well, actually, I believe that Rebecca Thompson is responsible for organising a lot of it. She volunteers for a lot of the Martha's Vineyard functions. She's very good at it from what I've seen. She used to be a party planner or wedding planner or something before her husband died; that was a while ago now. He left her a ton of money so she pretty much retired too. That's the island scuttlebutt anyway. So? How's JAWSfest?"

"Well, I haven't seen a lot of it. What I have seen was pretty cool. I'm not entirely sure why it is that I got my V.I.P. bracelet though. The general admission bracelet was fifty bucks and mine was three hundred!

Next time I will not be spending it on a gold plastic bracelet. I'll spend it on enjoying the island." Charles finished the salad and put it on the table.

"Oh, this guy showed up yesterday at the Newes pub. I used to get him confused with Karl Bass actually. I doubt I will anymore. His name is Tim Oakes. He worked on JAWS back in 1974. He's an islander but he went back to Hollywood to eke out a career there; I think he's a carpenter. Anyway, to hear him tell it you'd think that he was Spielberg himself! My friends all eat up his stories but the guy makes me puke."

"As long as steak doesn't make you puke." Laurie held up two beautiful rib eyes. "Come on out to the back deck with me and let's put these bad boys on the grill!"

The two friends moved out to the back deck and Laurie threw the steaks on the barbeque. Charles went back in and grabbed the two bottles of wine. He topped up Laurie's glass and then his own. They sat in quiet soaking up the sun and watching the ocean.

"Do you ever think about going back to Toronto?" Charles asked perched on the railing looking at the sea.

"Nope." Laurie was leaning back in an unfinished Adirondack chair with her eyes closed.

"Toronto is a great city." Charles said.

"Yes, it is."

"You wouldn't leave the Vineyard?"

"Not for anything."

There was a long pause. "I don't blame you."

17

Charles woke up in his bed at The Edgartown Inn feeling well rested and happy. It was amazing how good a quiet night with a good friend could make you feel, he thought. In Charles' book, it didn't get much better than barbequed steak, potatoes, and salad. For dessert, Laurie had surprised him with home-baked butter tarts that she had baked that morning. Charles wondered where she got the time but Laurie said that baking relaxed her. She had made half of them with raisins and half of them plain. She said that she could never decide which one she preferred so she always baked both. Charles preferred raisins but would take butter tarts any way that he could get them. They had sat out on the deck until quite late, drinking wine, and laughing. They brought up old stories from high school and ex-boyfriends and girlfriends whom they had both long forgotten. The best thing about getting old was having friends who had known you for a long time. Charles was delighted to have bumped into Laurie again. He had forgotten how beautiful she was. He got up and got dressed. The sun was bright again and the sheer white curtains gave everything a soft ethereal light. It was warm and comforting. He looked out the window; the streets were quiet, just the usual morning traffic of joggers, sailors, and coffee drinkers. Charles thought that coffee sounded like a fine idea. He grabbed his room key and went out into the inn.

Charles shut his room door behind him to find Edie standing in the doorway to the kitchen. She was dressed in another black dress; he really wanted to say something to her about that. She was so pretty. She would do well to brighten up her wardrobe a bit. As dark as her wardrobe was, she greeted him with one of her warmest smiles. "Good morning! It's not even seven yet; you *are* an early riser. Coffee?"

"Yes please." Charles walked over to her and reached out for the same American flag mug that he had the last time.

"Just a little milk, right?" Edie looked at him happily.

Charles looked down into the mug. His coffee looked perfect. "Absolutely. Thank you Edie."

"I told you I'd get it before you left." She returned the pot to the burner in front of her. "Go ahead and take that out to the porch and I'll check you for a refill in a few minutes."

"Oh, you don't have to do that, Edie."

"I don't mind. You're the only one up anyway and probably will be for quite some time."

"Alright. Thank you very much." Charles walked out to the porch and sat down on the same lounger that he had sat on the previous morning. He was a creature of habit and always had been. Charles found that if he maintained some sort of structure in his life, it left his mind open to think about other things. He didn't want to spend his time thinking about silly things like what to wear or what to eat. There were always more important, certainly more interesting things to think about. He was thinking about Rebecca Thompson now. Was she the one sleeping with Sean Burroughs? He was very handsome in that dark brooding way. He was fit. She was very attractive as well. He was also a lot younger than she was; however, she didn't seem like the cougar type. Sean definitely seemed like the type to be into cougars. Cougars were a hot ticket these days with younger men. When Charles had been younger it was still taboo but nowadays, older women were definitely seen as a feather in a young man's cap. Same old double standard though, the young man was a stud, the older woman was a bit of a tramp. This shoe didn't seem to fit Rebecca. She didn't seem like she was on the prowl at least not for young jocks. Charles saw her as more of a 'trolling for older millionaires' type. It might not be her. All they had to go on was perfume but that was a hell of a coincidence and Charles didn't believe in coincidences. Rebecca Thompson wore Lolita Lempicka- that much was certain. Sean Burroughs' pillow and closet also smelled of Lolita Lempicka.

Rebecca Thompson was the JAWSfest co-ordinator and Sean Burroughs' twin brother, Mike, was the biggest JAWS fan going. They would have met for sure. After all, Mike's collection was on display at the festival. Yep, Charles thought, too many coincidences.

Edie came out on to the porch with a coffee pot in her right hand and a newspaper in her left. "Top up?" Without waiting for a response, Edie filled Charles' cup that was sitting on the glass topped, white wicker table between them.

"Thank you."

"I also thought that you might like to see this." She handed him the paper. "This is what that terrible business across the street was about the other day. Breaks my heart." She put the paper down and motioned across the street. "This will probably put the shark attack out of everyone's mind. That's probably a good thing." She suddenly looked stricken. "Oh! I don't mean that it's good that the poor boy is dead, I just mean that, well..." Edie blushed.

"You mean that if there was going to be a bright side, that would be it." Charles smiled.

"Exactly. Thank you. You must think I'm terrible." Edie shook her head.

"Not at all." Charles picked up the paper. "Anything to get the shark attack out of people's heads is good as far as I'm concerned. I don't want people mass-murdering sharks. It really upsets me."

"I kind of feel the same way. I mean, look at it from the sharks' perspective- if a total stranger jumped into my living room in their underwear, I'd attack them too!" With that, Edie went back to the kitchen.

Charles opened the paper. The front page read, "OFF-ISLANDER MURDERED IN EDGARTOWN HOTEL". They really go for the gold, don't they? Charles thought. Jerks. Edie was right though. This would wash away any thoughts of Great Whites picking off tourists on State Beach. Someone picking off tourists in the heart of Edgartown was far more exciting and frightening.

North Water Street was quiet at that time of the morning and Charles walked the street unaffected by traffic. Past captain's houses, green trees, and huge hydrangeas, Charles headed toward Fuller Street Beach for his morning swim. Captain Hurtubise had said that there were no signs of Great Whites in the water and the one that got Karl Bass had definitely been baited. Surely, it would not have been interested in bathers without the encouragement of a little homemade chum. Charles was sure that it was long gone. Still, he had made sure to sneak past Edie with his swimming gear. She would have blown a gasket if she had known that he was heading back into the ocean. He had promised. When he got to the end of the Street, he turned right, down through the brush, and on to the path to the beach. The path itself was sandy and short and could very well be considered part of the actual beach. It probably wasn't though, thought Charles, but rather an access path to the docks for the hotel at the top of the hill. There were a few of them a long the way with large wooden gates fastened with signs that read, 'PRIVATE DOCK Please Keep Off'. Each sign was kind of cool in its rusticity and Charles took a picture of one with his iPhone. He passed the Edgartown lighthouse, Charles' second favourite lighthouse on the island after the Gay Head Lighthouse, and walked down the beach to the same spot he had chosen the previous morning. There was a warm breeze encouraging the waves to lap quietly at the sand. It was another perfect morning. Charles dropped his towel and his T-shirt on the sand and kicked off his flip-flops. Without giving himself time to second-guess his actions, he waded quickly into the water and dove in. It was cool without being jarring. The heavy salt water seemed to pull him away from shore, carrying him in his breaststroke along the water's surface. Charles remembered reading that Katharine Hepburn swam in the ocean every morning when she was in Connecticut right up until the end. He could understand why. It seemed to Charles like a cure-all. Nothing could be wrong if you had started your day swimming in the ocean. As he swam, he watched sailboats go by on the horizon and gulls dipping for breakfast. There were a couple of people on the beach but none of them were swimming nor were they even dressed for it. They had brought their towels but they were all wearing shorts and tank tops not their suits. He continued to swim out from the beach. He was much further out than he had been the day before. The water was so beautiful. He plunged under the surface and swam completely submersed and came up with a gasp completely exhilarated. He was out too far. He scanned the beach and noticed that the others had gone. He was alone. There was no one to help him if he got into trouble. Charles wasn't sure what anyone could do in an emergency but it wasn't safe anyway. Charles headed in. A cold current rushed over him and Charles wondered why. Had something pulled a current of water passed him? Was something checking him out? There was no way of knowing. All he could do was keep swimming. Another current of water swept passed him, under him. He definitely felt like he wasn't alone. The water was dark and the early morning sun was bright and low in his eyes. He couldn't see anything. Charles kept swimming. His breathing was laboured; he was swimming hard. He was further out than he had thought. The tide had pulled him out quickly but it was working against him now. If he wanted to hit shore, the ocean was going to make him work for it. Charles kicked as hard as he could and the beach got closer. He stood up about ten feet from the beach and turned around as fast as he could not exactly sure what he expected to see. For a split second, there was a flash in the water thirty feet from where he stood- a flash of water going across the current. Was it a fin? Changing course? It looked like the tip of a black fin flashing as it headed back out to sea. Was it his imagination? Charles watched the surface for any sign of life. Nothing. He waded back to shore.

170

*　　*　　*

"I shouldn't feed you a crumb for breakfast!" Edie shook her finger at him in the dining room doorway and there was no sign of her usual broad smile.

"Why?" Charles was shocked at his reception.

"You went swimming this morning and don't try and tell me that you didn't!" She guided him outside to the same table he'd had last time and when he sat down she smacked him on the head semi-playfully.

"Alright, I did but I don't think that I'll be doing *that* again, not after today." Charles ordered the same breakfast he had the morning prior.

Edie sat down across from him. "Why? Did something happen?" There was genuine concern on her face.

Charles told her the story about feeling a presence in the water and feeling current swish past him in an opposite direction of the current he was in.

"It could have been undertow. Some of the beaches get a pretty strong one sometimes but there were no waves of any sort? That's usually a pretty quiet beach." She thought about it some more. "Well, it could have been a school of bluefish. That's always possible. There are tons of fish in these waters. In fact, one of them is the Great White Shark so that's a possibility too! You'd better watch yourself!" She shook her head disapprovingly. "I'll get your breakfast." Edie got up and strode toward the kitchen. She brought back a piece of that delicious coffee cake and Charles sank his teeth in.

Charles was halfway through his breakfast when he got a text from the Chief. It read, "Be there in 10". He finished wiping up his eggs with freshly baked bread, asked for a coffee to go, and went back to his room to wash up. Charles was on the veranda when the police cruiser pulled up. He walked down the steps to the street and pulled open the car door. Before he could get in there was a holler from the inn.

"Chief! Chief Knickles!" Edie came down the stairs with the coffee pot that seemed permanently fixed in her right hand and a paper to-go cup in the other.

"Hi Edie! What can I do you for?"

"Oh, I'm fine Chief. I just thought that you might want a coffee. You're probably drinking cold coffee from yesterday. Am I right?"

The chief laughed, "as a matter of fact, you are right." She reached out of her window for the fresh cup. "Thank you very much, Edie. That's much appreciated. Saves me a stop."

"My pleasure. Give me the old cup there and I'll throw it out." Edie took the old cup from the Chief and turned to leave but thought better of it and turned back around. "Oh, and Chief..."

"Yes?"

"Do something about your friend here! He won't listen to me. Tell him to stay out of the god-damned water until you get everything sorted over that attack at State Beach."

Laurie turned to Charles. "You went swimming this morning?"

"*...And yesterday morning!*" Edie shook her head.

"You went swimming yesterday too before we even talked to Captain Hurtubise?"

"Thanks Edie. You've been a big help." Charles rolled his eyes and got in the car.

"That'll teach you to lie to me." She winked at him from the chief's window. "Have a nice day you two." Edie walked back inside as they drove off. "Go catch some bad guys!"

"I can't believe you went swimming!" Laurie turned on him incredulously.

"You heard the captain! There are no sharks around...probably."

"You're insane." Laurie shook her head and took a mouthful of coffee. "That Edie makes a fine cup of coffee."

"Her breakfasts are out of this world too."

"You don't have to tell me. I've had a few. That coffee cake is serious business."

Charles nodded his agreement. "Are we headed to Rebecca Thompson's house?"

"Rebecca Thompson's and Correllus State Forest- I hope you're up for a hike!" Laurie turned and grinned at him.

Charles looked down at his footwear; he was wearing running shoes. "I hope I am too."

The Chief drove the cruiser through Edgartown waving at locals periodically as she passed. Being the Chief of Police made you something of a celebrity if you did your job right, thought Charles. Everyone should know who the Chief was and as far as Charles could tell, they did. They drove up Main Street past the Old Whaling Church and finally turned left on to Edgartown West Tisbury Road. This was the same route to Karl Bass's house, thought Charles. Trees surrounded them. He couldn't tell whether or not they were Pitch Pine or Scrub Oak but the Chief seemed to be up on that. Charles found botany very interesting and was eager to learn. He made a mental note to buy a textbook or two when he got home. They drove in quiet for quite a distance enjoying the morning and the scenery. The car radio was on MVY Radio; the song was 'Lowdown' by Boz Scaggs. It was a good song. Charles recognised the disc jockey from listening to the iPhone app. Martha's Vineyard danced past his window as he drank his coffee and it filled him with a feeling of contentment that he rarely felt in the big city. The scenery on the island changed from moment to moment: beaches, forests, harbours, historic villages, but it never stopped being beautiful. Charles wondered what it would be like to live there full-time. Would he get to the point where he took it for granted? Charles doubted it. He wasn't the type of person that took things for granted as it was. Charles thought that the people who took things for granted didn't suffer from overexposure but rather a lack of imagination. They needed to look inside and retrain themselves to see life again. Charles just saw it as another form of negativity. Someone was either a negative person or a positive person; it was a choice but positivity took more work.

The cruiser slowed and turned right on to Bold Meadow Road. The houses were newer and quite pristine. Definitely over the million-dollar price range easy, he thought. The Chief pulled into the driveway of a white Greek revival home with a two-storey, grey shingle barn. Charles could tell from the white side door that the second storey of the garage was a guesthouse. It was actually quite common for island properties to have a second building for boats, cars, visitors, and most importantly- renters.

"Rebecca Thompson's?" Charles looked out of the windshield at the immaculate home.

"Easy genius, you don't want to use up all of your smart juice on little things like this. Save it for the big stuff." The Chief winked at her friend.

"I don't remember you being this sarcastic." Charles grinned and shook his head. "Your job has left you scarred and jaded."

They got out of the car and closed the doors in unison. The front door of the house opened and Rebecca Thompson stepped out onto the side porch of her home. "Chief, Mr Williams, what brings you out this way?"

The Chief looked over at Charles and back at Rebecca. "You remember Mr Williams from JAWSfest, Rebecca?"

"I do, actually, yes but it's also a very small island, Chief. Word gets around." Ms Thompson smiled and Charles wondered if her allergies were still bothering her. Rebecca's eyes were still red and puffy but upon closer inspection, Charles thought that it looked more like she had been crying than hay fever. The Chief shot him a quick, knowing look and Charles knew that she had come to the same conclusion.

"What word is that exactly?"

"That you are investigating the death of the young man in Edgartown and that your friend, here, is assisting you. No one is really sure of his credentials to do so but he seems pleasant enough and word has it that he is very smart, that he is here for JAWSfest, and that he is staying at Edie's place- The Edgartown Inn."

"The pipeline has served you well, Rebecca." The Chief laughed. "It's hard to keep a secret on this little island but we have some questions we'd like to ask you if that's alright."

"Certainly. Please come in. I'll put on some tea. I have some orange tea biscuits with raisins that I made this morning if you're interested." Rebecca turned to walk into the house and the Chief and Charles followed her in.

The home was beautiful. It looked like a showroom. Charles always wondered how people managed to live in homes like this. Nothing ever looked sat on or used. Did Rebecca Thompson and her ilk run around fluffing pillows and hiding dirty plates when someone drove up the drive or did they just stand in the middle of the kitchen in a freshly pressed dress like a Stepford Wife waiting for someone to show up? It seemed unfathomable to him. The walls were painted in that sandy colour that was so popular; Charles remembered his own paint was called 'Natural Linen'. The trim was a polar bear white. All of the furniture was in shades of brown. It was immaculately put together but it came off as a house not a home. That made Charles a little sad. Rebecca led them into the kitchen and motioned for them to sit at the glass kitchen table. Charles figured that this was where Rebecca spent most of her time. It was easily maintained leaving the rest of the house for show. Charles and the Chief sat down and Rebecca filled the electric kettle from the kitchen tap. She plugged it in.

"What would you like to talk about Chief?" Rebecca asked.

"I'd like to ask you about your relationship with Sean Burroughs."

There was a long pause and even though Rebecca's back was to the Chief and to Charles, they could see her body go limp at the mention of his name. "Sean...Burroughs?" She tried to ask like she didn't recognise the name but her voice was weak and her shoulders started to shake. She began to cry. With her left hand she brought a hanky to her face and with her right she opened the cupboard door and tried awkwardly to get down the tea. "I'm sorry...I'm sorry."

The Chief stood up, walked over to her, and guided her to a chair at the glass table. She sat down. The Chief let her cry for a few minutes. When Rebecca calmed down a little, the Chief spoke, "Why don't you tell us about you and Sean?"

Rebecca nodded meekly. "I met Sean last summer when he and his brother came to the island for vacation. His brother wanted to come on some sort of pilgrimage and since they don't have any other family, Sean came with him. They always tried to take vacations together. The year before, they had gone to California I believe; Sean was a surfer, so he chose the West Coast. Last year Mike picked Martha's Vineyard for the whole JAWS thing. He was a bit of a player...Sean not Mike. I was at Nancy's in Oak Bluffs with some of my girlfriends, not our usual sort of place but somehow we had ended up there and I met Sean. It was definitely Sean's sort of place. My tastes are usually more champagne and caviar while Sean's were more beer and burgers." She shook her head and smiled with memories. "We had such a good time." The kettle started to whistle. Rebecca went to stand but the Chief stopped her; she was on a roll.

"Charles will get that. Please continue," said the Chief.

Charles heard the command and sprung up to get the tea.

"Oh, okay. The mugs and teapot are to the left of the fridge," said Rebecca.

"Thank you." Charles found the mugs and teapot in the cupboard specified. There also a large pile of brown envelopes wedged in the side of the cupboard. Charles looked over his shoulder at the table where he had left the others. Rebecca's back was to him; he took a quick look through them.

"We spent most of his two weeks on the island together, the evenings anyway." Rebecca continued. She blushed at the mention of the evenings and what it implied. She looked at the Chief. "What you must think of me."

"Why?" The Chief looked at her comfortingly. "It sounds lovely."

"Chief, I know I look good but I don't look *that* good. There was almost a twenty year age difference." Rebecca lowered her head at the mention of age.

"So? I should be so lucky." The Chief straightened up as Charles came over with the tea. He poured a mug for each of them and sat down.

"I don't see a big deal either Ms Thompson." Charles sipped his tea. It was vanilla rooibos tea, his favourite. "For what it's worth."

"Of course you don't; you're a man. It's different for women."

"Let's get back on track here." The Chief reached for Rebecca's arm. "What happened next?"

"He left. They left. I didn't really expect to see him back this year but we kept in touch with emails and phone calls and when the summer came around, he wanted to come back to the island to see me. I was thrilled. Except for some reason, he didn't want his brother to know. That upset me a little."

"Do you know why?"

"Not exactly. I know that their parents were long dead and there were no cousins or aunts and uncles. They were all that they had- twins at that. Sean was very grounded especially for his age but Mike was younger emotionally. I think Sean felt that Mike would find it threatening if he were in a serious relationship. Sean told me that he told Mike that he was always with different women when he was with me. How sad. Anyway, they came back. Mike was thrilled as you can imagine what with JAWSfest being here." She sipped her tea. She seemed a lot calmer now.

"So it was you who was with Sean the night he was murdered." The chief continued.

"Yes. Mike was out at the festival and Sean met me at Nancy's for supper and a drink. Funny, I always hated Nancy's but then it became our place and I rather like it now. People can really have an effect on you can't they?" She smiled blankly. "I drove him back to his hotel. It was early so we felt safe enough to go upstairs which we've never done before. He always came back here. Lord those boys were messy. I guess living without a mother…"

The Chief and Charles looked across the table at each other.

"Rebecca, did you see anyone when you left? Anyone on the street? Hovering at the door? A bellman? Anyone?"

She thought for a moment. "No, I'm sorry."

"That's alright. Rebecca, I apologise up front for the personal nature of this question but I have to ask. Did you and Sean use condoms?"

Rebecca didn't flinch. "Yes, we did. Why?"

"We believe that a condom was thrown in the waste basket and then removed. Would you know anything about that?"

"Yes, I threw it out in habit but remembered that Mike would be returning to the room. I, then retrieved it, rolled it in bathroom tissue and threw it away in a garbage bin outside."

"Alright. Well, thank you very much Rebecca. I'm sorry for your loss. If there's anything that I can do for you or if you think of anything else please let me know." The Chief stood and Charles did as well. They walked toward the front door. "The weather has been beautiful! Maybe some fresh air would do you good; a hike in Correllus State Forest perhaps? That would make you feel better." Once outside, Chief Knickles turned and looked at Rebecca who stood on her porch to see them off.

"No thank you. I spent my childhood in that forest. I've had enough. I'm more of a reading in the yard kind of girl these days. Thank you Chief. It was good to see you. Oh! You didn't get any tea biscuits!"

"Gives me a reason to come back and check how you're doing. Take care, Rebecca." The Chief and Charles got in the car and they drove down the long drive.

Once back on Edgartown West Tisbury Road, the Chief turned to Charles, "What do you think?"

"We now have more questions than answers!" Charles stated.

"Such as?"

"Who cleaned the Burroughs' boys hotel room? That was not the room of slobs. It looked like my Nana had been through there."

"Agreed."

"Did Mike know that Sean in effect had a girlfriend? If he did and he felt threatened enough..."

"Possible."

"In the cupboard, I found a ton of past due bills and unpaid lines of credit. Rebecca Thompson is really deep in debt. Money is always a good motive for murder but if it's the motive in this case, I can't see how."

"Me neither." The Chief thought. "Funny though, she doesn't live like a woman with financial problems."

"You would know better than I would."

The Chief pulled over at the side of the road and turned off the ignition. Charles looked around and then looked at the Chief, puzzled. There was nothing in sight except a big metal gate and a dirt path.

"Welcome to Manuel F. Correllus State Forest."

18

According to Laurie, Manuel F. Correllus State Forest was forty-three square miles of grasslands, woodlands, heathlands, and pine barren; Charles didn't know exactly what it was that made the four terms distinct but she did. The thickest part of the park was the pine barren on the southeast corner. The Chief figured that they would start there. Not only was it the most likely place to kill someone as it tended to be the densest part of the bush but it was also the closest part of the state forest to the homes of Karl Bass and Rebecca Thompson. At the foot of the each path around the park, there was a large iron gate built to keep out motor vehicles. Horses, bikes, and pedestrians were allowed to come and go as they pleased. The Chief and Charles swung their legs over the gate and stepped inside. They headed up the well-worn path. Hiking through the woods was actually a beautiful way to spend the day. Charles was happy for the exercise. Other than his brief morning swims, Charles had spent his vacation thus far in a police car, in a bus, or in a bar! He wasn't going to stay fit that way. The Chief stopped and looked back the way they had come and then looked forward again. She looked off into the woods and said, "This ought to do it. Let's go." She headed off the path and into the forest.

"Where are we?" Charles asked.

"I figure that if we cut a straight line through the pine barren from this point, we'd hit Karl Bass or Rebecca Thompson's place. I don't know where else to start. What do you think?" The Chief kept marching. Forging a path as she went through the thick bush.

"Seems like a logical place to start." Charles pressed on behind her. "So what exactly is a pine barren?"

"A pine barren is a plant community that occurs in fairly infertile soils and is dominated by grasses, wildflowers, shrubs, and medium sized pines. They also quite often contain scrub oak like this one." Laurie reached out and patted a tree as she passed it. The trunk of the tree had branched off into several stalks and the leaves were small and shiny like holly. Charles stopped to inspect it briefly. It was very interesting and the Chief was right, it was everywhere in the barren.

"You said there were pine barren, grassland, woodland, and heathland in this forest; what's a heathland?"

"A heathland is like a moor only not as peaty. That's the easiest way to explain it."

"Interesting."

"It's nice to be explaining something to you for a change." The Chief had her back to Charles but he could hear her grinning.

"I love learning new things. See? Everyone's happy. You should teach me things more often."

"Yeah, right! Talk about coals to Newcastle."

"I don't think that your analogy quite works but I appreciate the sentiment. Thank you. You are too kind." Charles kept slugging through the woods even though the underbrush was slicing his bare legs. They walked a while in silence. His next murder was going to have to happen in the middle of town. "Laurie?"

"Yes?"

"What's it like here in the winter?"

"Quiet."

"No really, what's it like to live here during the off-season?"

Laurie came to an abrupt halt and turned around. Charles almost slammed right into her. "What's wrong? What's the matter?" Charles stood tall and looked around.

"*Are you thinking of moving to the Vineyard from Toronto?*" The shock left an imprint on Laurie's face like she'd been jammed in the face with a cattle prod.

"Well, not exactly. I'm just thinking about what it would be like to move to the Vineyard. There's a subtle difference but a difference just the same. Jesus."

"Oh." The Chief turned and started hiking again. "Well, it's very different from on-season but in some ways, still the same."

"Great. That answers everything, doesn't it? Cleared everything up for me."

"Will you hold on? I wasn't finished yet and just for the record, you have your fair share of sarcastic moments yourself!" Laurie laughed.

"Oh well, I'm sorry. Please continue." Charles said.

"Well, everything that you love about the island is still there only more so. You know what I mean? The tourists are great; they bring a lot of money to the island without which we couldn't survive and for the most part, they are very well behaved and happy. The island does that to people, as you well know; however, the tourists also bring with them the outside world. Any hints of America that you see or feel are because of the tourists. When they leave, so does America in a way. A lot of the shops and businesses close up and think about it- eighty per cent of our population leaves! That's huge. Maybe you don't realise it because you come from a really big city but to us, the summer is quite congested."

She was right. Charles didn't think that the island was particularly congested. It was busy sure enough but certainly not to the point where it was uncomfortable or remarkable in any way. Downtown Toronto was much worse.

"The island slows down, Charles. There are a lot of beautiful quiet walks on beaches but wearing a jacket instead of a T-shirt. The ocean gets cold but stays stunning. Winters here are beautiful. It's a great place for Christmas."

"That would be nice."

"It would be nice having you here." The Chief did not look back but her voice softened slightly with sincerity.

"Would it?" Charles felt his cheeks blush slightly.

Laurie stopped and turned around. "Of course it would. I still feel like somewhat of an outsider here. Don't get me wrong, the people are great but they're islanders or they're faking it really well. I love it here and it is my home but I just haven't felt secure in the fact that there was someone on my side. That is..." she tapered off and sat down on a tree stump.

"...Until I got here?" Charles smiled.

"Yes." Laurie couldn't meet his gaze.

"Laurie, I have enjoyed our time together on this island more than I have enjoyed spending time with anyone in a very long time." Charles reached down and touched her hand. She took it. "I don't think that it's all because of the corpses and the sharks either." They both laughed. Charles was good at breaking the tension with humour. "But I'd be lying to you if I said that I knew exactly what I was feeling because I don't."

"I don't really know either and I probably shouldn't have brought it up." Laurie smiled an unguarded smile and she looked beautiful in the filtered sunlight. "We should keep going." She stood up and her pants were filthy.

"You have crap all over your pants." Charles started brushing her off.

"Oh sure! You don't know what you are feeling but you think you can grab my ass in the woods!" Laurie laughed. "Am I good to go now?"

"Hold on. Your pants are covered in something and it's not the tree." Charles looked at the black substance on his hand and then inspected the tree stump. There was a large black spot on a broken jagged piece of bark on the stump. It was dry and had soaked into the porous wood but it had been a liquid of some sort.

"Hold on a second." Laurie produced a test tube from her breast pocket and popped open the lid. She then produced a swab from inside and wiped the blackened area of the stump. Replacing the swab in the test tube, the results were instant. The vial turned pink. "It's blood."

19

"Hey! What's going on?" Larry grabbed Charles by the neck and dragged him over to the bar at Seasons in Oak bluffs.

"Oh, hey man." Charles smiled at his friend. Larry was standing at the bar waiting for his order while the rest of the JAWSfest crew were at a nearby table. Charles wanted a Guinness- it had been quite a day. He turned toward the bartender and once he got her attention, he ordered his stout.

"I know you're in tight with the cops; what is the story with Mike's brother Sean? Shot in his room! None of us can believe it! That's messed up mate." Even when he was talking about a murder, Larry's accent made it sound good to Charles.

"Well, I'm not sure that I can tell you more than anything you have probably already read in the papers. We don't really know all that much. He was shot in his hotel room, probably while he was sleeping." Charles paid for his beer, tipped the bartender, and walked back to the table with Larry. "What do you know about Karl Bass?"

"From JAWS, you mean?" Larry said. "Not that much really. Just what we've all read on Facebook. He was originally an islander but he worked on the movie, you know. Have you asked Oakes? He must know him. They were both islanders, they're both about the same age, and they went back with production. I don't see how they could not know each other."

Charles cringed at the name. "Yeah, you're probably right. I just hate the thought of talking to that guy. He's full of two things- himself and bullshit and I don't care for either one."

Larry laughed, "that's true enough but he might be able to help you out about Karl. Why the interest anyway?"

Charles thought long and hard about what he was going to say next. He hated lying but he didn't think that he should be spreading information after Laurie had put such faith in him either. Larry seemed to pick up on this.

"Don't sweat it mate. You can't tell me. I respect a man who can keep his word. One day, after all of this is over, you and I will sit down and talk this whole thing through over a pint and a good fish and chips." Larry grinned at his friend.

"That's the best offer I've had since I got here. You're on." Charles was thankful for Larry's thoughtfulness. He was a good guy. The two of them

190

reached the table of friends sitting in the back corner like they had been when Charles had met them on that first night. It seemed an eternity ago. So much had happened. This had definitely been the most exciting vacation that he had ever been on. Charles thought that might be gruesome to say but it was true. JAWS, Laurie Knickles, Larry and the JAWS gang, a shark attack, murder, a police investigation, and let's not forget the island itself, Martha's Vineyard. Hiking through the forest this morning with Laurie had been amazing! Discovering blood on the stump in the woods? Who would have thought that was even possible? Charles couldn't wait to find out what the results were from the official scan of the area. After they had made their discovery, they made their way back to the Chief's cruiser and called Detective Jeff. Jeff came out with two other officers who went back into the forest with Laurie. Jeff had driven Charles back to the Edgartown Inn before returning to assist in the search. Charles was very sad that Sean and Karl had passed away and he was terribly sorry for how hurt Mike Burroughs was but there was a level of fascination in the goings on around the tragedy that was not so much appealing per se, as it was exciting. He sat down with Brooke on his left, who greeted him with her usual kiss and hug, and her brother Larry sat down on Charles' right. "So how's JAWSfest treating everyone today, guys?"

"I don't know why you bothered to get yourself a VIP pass, Charles. You're barely using the bleeding thing!" Brooke took a sip of her pint. "The festival has been excellent though. I'm having a brilliant time! I never want to go back!" Brooke always seemed to be giggling when she talked. Because it was genuine, it was an endearing quality.

"It has been pretty cool man. You're missing a good time." Tim's Georgian drawl gave him a permanent laid back sound; however, he was a full-fledged Pink Floyd fan and as far back as Charles could remember he had never met a hyper Floyd fan. "I've been getting a lot of cool discussions going. That Jeffrey Kramer is a really down to earth guy and the ladies are pretty awesome. Susan Backlinie man, I wish I could take her home. She's just awesome. They never make you feel like they're rushing you. They're getting a pretty good gig out of it, I suppose though. A paid vacation on the Vineyard man, I'd take it." Tim nodded his head.

All of a sudden Charles was grabbed from the back by a hand on either shoulder. "Holy Shit!" He screamed.

"Hey buddy, that Chief chick is hot!! Are you tapping that?" Andy squatted behind Charles oblivious that he had scared him. "Chicks in uniform make me hot."

"Andy! You sod! You don't ask him a question like that!" Brooke smacked Andy on the side of the head. "Jesus Christ, you're a bloody wanker, you are!"

"You're damned right I am. I'm wanking every morning! God didn't make me wake up with a hard-on for no reason. You've got to make sure everything is still working so you know that there's a reason to get out of bed in the morning! Am I right?"

Charles nodded his head in agreement. "The wanker has a point."

Brooke laughed. "You guys are all out of your heads!"

"I'd have to agree with that too." Larry chimed in.

"Jesus Christ, I don't want to hear about it from my bloody brother! That's an image I don't need."

"Now you know why he took so long in the shower in the mornings when you were growing up!" Andy elbowed Brooke and winked at her playfully.

"Is that true? Christ! I stood in that bloody shower! Our mum stood in that shower- Jesus, she still does!!"

"Dad didn't exactly take short showers either." Larry had an innocent face on him and didn't meet her gaze.

"I'm going to be sick." Brooke laughed until tears were coming out of her eyes.

This distraction was exactly what Charles needed. He looked across the table at Eddie and Tina Simms and Jackie Lewis; they were deep in conversation with their heads over a newspaper. "Hey! Jackie, what are you guys talking about so intensely over there?"

Jackie's blonde hair fell around her face as she turned to Charles. "Anything but British masturbators." She rolled her eyes disapprovingly but smiled at him nonetheless. "We're going over the schedule of events for tomorrow. Are you joining us?"

"Well, I always plan to go to the festival; that's why I'm here after all but then I get called away." Charles wasn't sure why he was defending himself but he was.

"I suppose. Well, we'd love to hang tomorrow." Jackie was trying to act casual but Charles could tell that she was a bit hurt that he hadn't spent much time with them. Charles and Jackie had made plans on Facebook to hang out at the festival; so far, that hadn't really happened.

"So would I. It is my every intention. Even if the police want me, I will tell them that they can't have me all day. Cool?"

"Cool."

Charles knew that everything was a conscious decision. Everyone made choices. They could dance around it as much as they wanted with terms like "I have to" or "such and such is making me" but when it all came down to it, everything was a choice. Charles had been abandoning the festival for police work. If he were in a position to tell his friends what had been happening, they would understand why. "So what is the schedule for tomorrow?"

Tina spread out the JAWSfest newspaper on the table so they could all see it. "Ok," she said. "Tomorrow, open all day from 9:30am to 8:30pm, is the *Sharks, Art, and Conservation Exhibit*. That's here

194

in Oak Bluffs. *Behind The Screams* and *JAWS Store* are open for the same amount of time at the Daniel Fisher House. *Living JAWS: Antics from Amity* is at Old Whaling Church from 9:30 to 11:30am but at the same time there is a meet and greet with event VIP's and Greg Nicotero. I haven't met him yet; I'd like to go to that." Tina looked up from the paper at the group.

"He's really cool. I love that *Walking Dead* show dude." Tim nodded as if in agreement with his own statement.

"I already know the *Antics from Amity*. I don't need to sit there and be told again about a drunken Murray Hamilton getting sprayed by a skunk." Tina shook her head and the group laughed. She kept reading from the paper. "After that, there's a meet and greet with event artists and authors. That sounds cool too. Then there's *Living JAWS: Fish Stories, In The Water With Great Whites*."

"Is Rodney Fox at that one? If he is, I am definitely going to that one." Charles smiled at the thought of one of his childhood heroes. Rodney was incredibly cool.

"Then there's *The Women of JAWS*, the one that Oakes was trashing. I think that sounds be great. They all held such different positions. It's not like they were all production secretaries or something. Lastly, there is the screening in Ocean Park of JAWS. That will be wicked!! Watching that outside by the beach? Awesome."

"It's a full day tomorrow! Sounds excellent. I will definitely be there for the screening." Charles stood up. "I'm going to get another beer; this waitress is terrible. Want to come with me?" he asked Larry.

"Sure thing mate. We'll order a round for the table and get them to send it back." Larry stood up with him and they made their way through the room. When they got to the bar, Charles noticed an argument in progress. It was between two men. One of them was the unmistakable Tim Oakes. Charles cringed. He wasn't sure what to do. He didn't want to draw attention to them in fear that Oakes would join them nor did he want to point the argument out to Larry and run the risk that Larry would call Oakes over to them. The group seemed to be under a certain spell cast by Oakes and Charles could not understand it for the life of him. Looking at Larry, he could see that it was too late; Larry had noticed Oakes and was watching the argument. Before either of them could say anything, the man sitting with Oakes jumped to his feet and punched Oakes across the jaw. Oakes fell back in his chair and landed on the floor. The bouncers who had been standing motionless by the door sprung into action at a pace that Charles would not have considered possible for men of their size. The two men grabbed the man who had punched Oakes and dragged him out of the bar. The waitress went over to Oakes and helped him to his feet. Oakes was a big man and had probably not been hurt but the waitress made a fuss over him. No question, Oakes was a good-looking man. Women were probably not a problem for him, thought Charles. Keeping a woman was probably a difficulty although it never ceased to amaze Charles what some woman would put up with in order to maintain a relationship. He watched as Oakes smiled at the waitress and placed a large meaty hand on her shoulder. He was right. Charles could tell by her body language that Oakes could have this one if he wanted her. She took out her pad and pen and wrote something down. She tore off a page and handed it to Oakes. Charles wanted to gag. It was then that Oakes saw them and waved at Larry. He headed their way. Why couldn't the bouncers have tossed him out too?

"Hey guys!" Oakes said as he came over.

"Hey." They said in unison although Charles sounded a little less enthusiastic than Larry did. Stupid bouncers, he thought.

"Where is everyone?" Oakes put his hand on Larry's shoulder. He stood about three inches taller than Larry and Charles' six feet.

"They're over here at the table. Come on over. Do you need to grab a beer?" asked Larry.

"No, that little blonde broad is bringing me one on the house for getting punched in the face." Oakes smiled with self-satisfaction. "Not bad really: I get tapped in the face by that fucking pussy- he gets tossed and I get free beer and a fuck from the waitress after her shift. I'd get punched by that moron every night if I knew that was going to be the deal." He laughed loudly at his own joke.

"Oakes!" Tim McKenna jumped up from his chair and shook Oakes' hand vigorously. "How's it goin' man?"

"I'm good buddy; I'm good." Oakes grabbed a chair from a neighboring table without asking and sat down.

"What have you been up to all day? I thought for sure we'd bump into you at some point at the festival!" Tim was definitely suffering from some sort of hero worship. Charles just couldn't understand it.

"Nah, fuck that man. They didn't want me speaking at their precious festival so, I couldn't be bothered." Oakes sneered.

"Well why come to the island then?" Charles challenged softly.

"The island's open to everyone is it not?" Oakes snorted. "I mean, is everyone here for fuckin' JAWSfest?"

"Of course not. I'm just saying that if they upset you so badly maybe you would have been happier coming to Martha's Vineyard on one of the other fifty one weeks of the year when there wasn't a JAWSfest. That's all." Charles maintained an innocent smile the entire time knowing full well that he was irritating Oakes. The man obviously wasn't used to being challenged.

Oakes stared at Charles carefully. Tension was building at the table; everyone could feel it. "I suppose that would make sense but unfortunately, I had some business to attend to this week. I have a lot of ties to the island."

"That's too bad."

"What's that supposed to mean? Who the fuck are you anyway?"

Tim and Larry jumped in. "Hey man! It's cool! This is Charles. He's a good guy! He's a buddy of ours! He didn't mean anything by it. Did you Charles? You didn't mean anything did you?"

"Certainly not. I just meant that it was too bad that he had to do business on the island at a time when there were so many people here whom he disliked." Actually, Charles had meant that it was too bad that Oakes had to come to the island when Charles was there and sour the festival but why start anything. People like Oakes never learned.

"See?" Tim said. "He didn't mean anything. Tell us a story from your days at Universal, man. You know so much shit. Come on man. Chill out and tell us a good one."

Oakes stared at Charles intensely and Charles continued to smile back innocently knowing that was what would piss him off the most. "Alright. If this guy will stop fucking riding me."

"It's all good." Charles said. "Please, I'd love to hear something about your days at Universal." This seemed to be more in line with what Oakes was used to hearing and it placated him somewhat. Still leery, Oakes started a story.

"Well, Al Wilde was a close friend. You remember Al? He was the bicycle shop owner and the guy at the beach. You know, 'that's some bad hat, Harry!' That guy! He was Harry. Well, the production was advertising for actors for the supporting roles in the film and at the time Al Wilde was directing and acting at the local theatre. He wasn't going to audition but I was already working on set under Joe Alves and I knew that they were having a tough time finding someone for the role of Harry Keisel. I knew Al would be perfect for it but he thought that he was too busy with the theatre and had no interest in the Hollywood types. One day I sat him down and talked to him. I was at the theatre touching up a set that Al had asked me to help him with and I said, 'Al, when are you going to get another opportunity like this? These people look up to you and would love to see you immortalized on screen. They need to have a record of your work to reflect on. Do it for the craft Al.' He went down the next day and they gave it to him on site. I was right; he was perfect for it."

Charles had never heard such garbage. 'Do it for the craft Al'? He almost lost it there. What was this guy trying to prove? He must have some real stories from the production that actually would be interesting. His ego was just too much. Charles knew from all of the reading and interviews that he had read and seen that Al Wilde was indeed the actor that had played Harry Keisel. Oakes had at least got that right; however, Mr Wilde had been active in the Martha's

Vineyard Little Theatre Group in the thirties and forties and had come out of his long retirement with an audition like everyone else. Charles doubted that Oakes was friends with Al Wilde. There would have been about a fifty-year age difference for starters. Sure he might have known him. The population of the island was about ten thousand at the time. Oakes probably did build sets for the theatre and that was how he ended up working for Universal but it would have been long after Al's involvement with them. By all accounts, Al was working at the post office by that point. Oakes' story was crap. Charles also found it interesting that someone who was so angry at the fact that JAWSfest had shown no interest in paying him to return as a speaker and who was just on the island at the same time as the festival by circumstance, loved nothing more than to sit and regale a captive audience with stories about JAWS. That was peculiar indeed. Charles figured that he would rather talk about anything but JAWS. Charles was debating whether or not to push the envelope by contradicting Oakes' story when the waitress that had given Oakes her number came up to the table. She was dressed in her street clothes.

"Hi Oakes!" She was a bouncy petite girl with blonde hair in a ponytail. "My shift is over!"

"Good shit, honey. Let's get out of here." Oakes got up from the table and grabbed her by the hand. He looked at the table of friends. "I don't know about you guys but Oakes isn't sleeping alone tonight!" He walked out of the bar almost dragging the girl behind him.

"That's a class act," said Charles. "Alright! So what are we doing tomorrow? I'm in for Rodney Fox for sure!"

20

"Mike Burroughs is out of the hospital." Laurie opened the conversation without a hello.

"That's excellent." Charles replied. "He must be doing a helluva lot better than the last time we saw him."

"I should think so. I'm going to go and talk to him. See what he can tell me."

"He can't be back at his hotel." Charles thought about it. "So, where is he staying?"

"Are you ready for this?" Laurie baited.

"I hope so."

"Rebecca Thompson's house."

"No kidding? Holy shit." Charles was genuinely surprised. "I didn't see that coming."

"Me either. Want to come with me? You may as well see this through to the end as bitter as it may be..."

"I *would* like that actually. I'd like to see this for myself." Charles thought for a minute. "There's a talk that I'd like to see at the festival though. I promised my friends that I'd be there. I'm starting to get a bit of frost from some of them for not hanging out a bit more. I'd like to see the *In The Water With Great Whites* lecture at the Old Whaling Church."

"I'm sure you would! As long as it's not instructional! When is it?"

"Noon to one-thirty."

"I'm heading out pretty soon. I can have you back for most if not all of it. How soon can I pick you up?" Laurie sounded distracted like people always do who multitask on the phone.

"I'm going to eat breakfast now and then I'll shower. I can be ready by eight-thirty."

"Well, take your time. I'm not heading out there until after nine or so. Rebecca is expecting me for ten."

"Alright. I'll be ready when you get here." Charles hung up the phone. Mike Burroughs was staying with Rebecca Thompson! He really hadn't seen that coming; however, if he thought about it, it sort of made sense. They were the two people mourning Sean's death more than anyone...and they did know each other. Where else was he going to go? There were definitely no available rooms on the Vineyard in the middle of August with such short notice. Everything had been booked up for months. Charles got dressed for breakfast. He had packed three pairs of shorts, five T-shirts, and two bathing suits. He was only planning to be there for five days and that seemed to be more than enough. He put on a pair of camouflage cargo shorts, a JAWS T-shirt, and his flip-flops. Grabbing his room key, he left for the dining room.

"I think that I'd be hurt at this point if you didn't stay here for breakfast!" Edie was standing outside his room at the half-door of the office when he came out. She walked over to the dining room and poured him a coffee. She added milk without asking and handed it to him. "I'll call you when we're good to go. You'll be on the porch?"

"Yes, thanks Edie." Charles took the coffee. It was in a different mug than the other mornings. This one was just as big as the other but it was a Martha's Vineyard tourist mug with a painting of the Edgartown Lighthouse on the side. Charles had seen them for sale in Oak Bluffs. He walked out onto the porch and sat down. He was curious about the morning ahead and what information Mike Burroughs might be able to give them about the death of his brother. Mike had been dealing with a lot of guilt when they last saw him. Charles found it hard to believe that all of that had subsided in such a short period. That is the kind of thing that was more likely to last for years. The more Charles thought about it, the more he thought that the morning ahead might be an uncomfortable one.

"You can come in for breakfast now, Charles." Edie stepped out on to the porch and hung the "Open for Breakfast" sign that she hung every morning. Charles had noticed that the breakfasts were quite popular with islanders. There were always a few locals who came in every morning. Charles could tell they were locals by the conversations that they would have with Edie and her staff. They talked about the schools, the famers' market, book sales, fundraisers, and specials at the Stop & Shop. Their familiarity with the island and each other could only come from years of living together in a small community. Charles liked the feeling. He went out back to his usual table in the garden and ordered the full breakfast; still not brave enough to order the stewed prunes, he went for the juice. The bread today was the usual white and the alternate was the cheese. He asked for a slice of each. After breakfast he returned to his room and had his shower. There were fresh towels like there were everyday and new soap. For all of its quaintness, the Edgartown Inn was very well run. Charles dressed again after his ablutions and took his iPad out on to the porch. He sat down on the chaise closest to the Edgartown Library so that he could tap into their Wi-Fi. There were a few things that he wanted to look up on the Internet. The first was Rebecca Thompson; the second was .40 caliber handguns.

*   *   *

Charles and the Chief stepped out of the car at the Thompson house and this time, she did not come out to meet them. They walked up to the house and the Chief knocked on the door. They weren't standing there long before Rebecca Thompson answered. She was fresh and neatly put together in a pair of dark jeans and a white dress shirt. She had on a string of pearls that added a sense of style. She smiled at them without a hint of the puffiness in her eyes that was so prevalent on their last visit. Her eyes were bright and her skin pink and smooth. "Good morning Chief, Mr Williams."

"Good morning Rebecca." The Chief answered. "We're here to speak to Mr Burroughs."

"Yes. Please come in." Rebecca stepped aside and the Chief and Charles stepped past her into the front hall. They both wiped their shoes on the mat and made their way into the kitchen. It was empty.

The Chief turned to look at Rebecca. "Where is he?"

"He's sleeping. He has been sleeping a lot. I'm not sure whether it's the drugs or depression. Only time will tell, I imagine. I'll wake him. Would you care for some tea?"

"That would be nice. Thank you." The Chief and Charles accepted her offer.

"This time you can have some tea biscuits. A fresh batch at that!" She walked over to a cake saver that was sitting on the counter and lifted the lid to reveal a beautiful stack of tea biscuits. "They're orange and raisin, my favourite."

"That's very considerate of you Rebecca but we're in a bit of a hurry; Charles has to be somewhere by noon."

"Oh, are you going to the *In The Water With Great Whites* talk with Rodney Fox?" Rebecca smiled at Charles.

"Um, yes. As a matter of fact, I am." Charles was a bit surprised that she knew where he was going.

"Don't look so surprised Charles; I made all of Mr Fox's travel arrangements and I organized the schedule for the festival. That was painstaking let me tell you! I know it backward and forward."

"Of course. Sorry, I forgot." Charles blushed slightly but not much.

"Rebecca? Mr Burroughs?" The Chief was persistent.

"Certainly. Right after I make your tea." She walked over to a cabinet and pulled down the kettle and teapot.

Charles stepped up. "Why don't I do that for you while you get Mr Burroughs? I made it last time; I know where everything is. It will give me something to do."

Rebecca stopped and for a minute, looked like she was going to argue but she relinquished. "Very well then. I'd appreciate that. I'll just go get my guest then, shall I?" Rebecca's smile was starting to look thin.

As soon as she left the room and Charles could hear her ascending the steps, he hurried over to the cabinet where he had seen all of the unpaid bills and opened it. The pile was still there but they were in a much more organized state and they were all stamped with a deep red 'PAID' rubber stamp. Bills that had been overdue for months were now laid to rest. Charles flipped through them quickly. "There are thousands and thousands of dollars worth of bills here. Almost one hundred thousand dollars! She's been borrowing from Peter to pay Paul for almost a year and now they were all paid yesterday."

"That is a little suspicious, especially under the circumstances. Money and love are always vying for the number one reason for murder. We have nothing to tie it to Rebecca though. We don't know where she got the money or what it would have to do with Sean Burroughs or Karl Bass. Mike and Sean aren't exactly the Vanderbilt's at least not that I can tell. It might be something separate all together. Her husband was a wealthy man. He would have left her a fortune. She could have just been cash poor for a while due to bad investments or maybe she's just one of those people who is notoriously bad at paying their bills on time. I certainly know my fair share of people like that and there's no law that says you have to be poor to be shitty with money."

"No that's true but I did some reading on Rebecca Thompson today. I don't think that she has as much money as you think she does. Her husband died and probably had a great insurance policy but other than that, he didn't leave her much. He had made some pretty bad investments before he died and got hit pretty hard. He's mentioned in the paper after the last market crash. I think that it almost wiped them out.

Now, that insurance would probably have been substantial but it wouldn't last forever- not with her tastes and travelling expenses. Not to mention keeping up living on the Vineyard. I would be very surprised if she was able to come up with this kind of money out of the blue and all at once." Charles filled and plugged in the teapot. Then he grabbed the vanilla rooibos tea from the other day and filled the infuser with loose leaf tea. The smell was gentle and smooth.

"Well maybe we need to talk to Rebecca a bit more." The Chief was deep in thought.

"What are we going to say, that every time we come over here we go through her cupboards and make shit up based on what we find? We have no idea what all this means but we should just keep it in mind." Charles put the bills back and closed the cupboard door.

"Fair enough." The Chief walked over to the kitchen table and sat down just as Rebecca returned to the kitchen followed by Mike Burroughs. He was groggy and disheveled but there seemed to be more life in him than there was when they saw him in the hospital. His hair was messy and his skin peaked but Charles was sure that was all due to the extra sleeping.

"Hi Charles. Good to see you. Thanks for coming over." Mike rubbed his eyes and sat down beside the Chief.

"My pleasure Mike. How are you holding up?" Charles walked over and patted his friend on the shoulder briefly.

"I'm alright. It's weird is all." Mike looked around the kitchen. "Is there anything to eat? I'm starving."

"Certainly, Michael. What would you like? There's homemade tea biscuits and marmalade. Why don't I bring those in for everyone when the tea is ready? Come, let's all move out into the sitting room." Rebecca ushered them out of the kitchen and into the pristine sitting room.

She sat Mike down in the chocolate brown club chair facing the window before hurrying back to the kitchen. Charles and the Chief got comfortable on the tan couch. It was a pleasant room if not personable. It was warm in colour but not in personality. There were no personal pictures that Charles could see and everything was immaculate. Charles liked a lived-in room, a room with signs of life and love. A room should say something about the person who lived in it. This room was so cold.

"Mike, tell me about your brother." The Chief sat forward and tried to speak as softly as she could while staying firm at the same time. Mike sat quietly but Charles could tell by watching him that he was not in the same comatose state that he had descended into in the hospital. The Chief must have recognised that too because she didn't press but rather waited patiently. They could see that Mike was collating his thoughts.

"Sean was my best friend." Mike said. "He knew me better than anyone and I knew him." Mike sat back and stared out the window not ten feet in front of him. "People talk about twins being closer than other siblings but I think it's one of those things. Unless you have a twin, there's no way of knowing exactly what it's like... I guess that's true of anything really."

"Probably." The Chief said. At this point she was just letting him talk.

"He had a lot of friends. He was very popular. He was so good-looking. Funny how that works isn't it? We were identical twins but he was much better looking than I am." Michael stared out the window. Charles couldn't see through it from where he and the Chief were sitting but he didn't think there was anything out there but trees. It was a quiet day. "It's true. Something about his demeanor, it made him more attractive. I have always been the hyper one where he was darker and brooding. That's always the more attractive quality."

"He was very attractive but so are you Michael." Rebecca walked back into the room and set down the biscuits and tea on the coffee table in the centre of the room. The Chief leaned in to take a biscuit on a small plate, as did Charles. Rebecca handed them each a mug of tea and a napkin.

"Thank you, Rebecca but you are just saying that. I appreciate it." Michael stayed in his chair and Rebecca brought him a biscuit and some tea. He took it but gave no sign of recognition. "He came with me to the Vineyard last year even though it was of no interest to him at all. It worked out all right for him in the end because he met Rebecca here. I wish he would have told me. I don't know why he felt he couldn't. I was his brother. I would have been so happy for him. I hated that he was jumping around form bed to bed. Turns out that he wasn't. I would have been so happy that he found someone kind." He looked at Rebecca whose eyes were tearing up again. Sitting in her chair across the room, she bowed her head in modesty but she said nothing. "Sean was funny... I can't believe it, you know?" Michael took a bite from his tea biscuit. He seemed to enjoy it more than he thought he would and he looked at it with mild surprise. They were delicious.

"There's something you should know." Michael said.

A single shot crashed through the bucolic silence of the Greek revival home. The picture window in the sitting room shattered. Another shot followed. It was loud and painful. It reverberated in their ears. Charles dropped instinctively to the floor, as did the Chief. Rebecca stood up and screamed. She screamed and screamed. "*Get down!*" The Chief yelled at her and she did as she was told. The Chief crawled over to the window. Charles saw Laurie's hands slicing on the broken glass but it didn't stop her. It couldn't be real. They were all watching a movie and it was on way too loud. Charles' ears hurt. He wanted to be sick; his heart was racing so fast. The Chief looked carefully out the window from the side but saw nothing. She turned and looked at Charles who was still motionless on the floor where he had fallen. There was tea and biscuits everywhere. In the middle of the room, still sitting in his chair was Michael. He didn't get down on the floor with the others. He didn't have time. He was frozen like a mask in a Halloween store. His right eye was gone and his face was glistening deep red. There was an explosion of black on his chest; the fabric of his shirt absorbed the blood as it continued to pump out of his heart. Soon his whole shirt was black from the chest down. He looked so surprised. He looked like a child who just didn't understand. The Chief started toward him but one more shot rang out and it told her to stay exactly where she was. There was nothing she or anyone else could do. They sat there and watched. They sat there and listened. They smelled the life leave Mike Burroughs' body. His one eye stared pleadingly at the Chief. His face changed colour. His body went limp. His eye stopped pleading but stared just the same. It seemed like an eternity sitting there, watching Mike die. His lap covered in shattered glass; his hair still messy and sticking up from his nap. Blood speckled the chair he sat in but there was none on the floor. After the life hissed out of him, all they could hear was Rebecca crying. She kept crying. No one moved for a very long time.

21

Charles sat in an examination room in the Martha's Vineyard Hospital. It was a very basic hospital room just like every other one he had ever seen. The walls were white and pale green. That pale green that human resources people always claimed that studies said was a soothing colour but real people said was nauseating. Charles had no patience for human resource people. They never got anything right. The walls were blank. The floor was blank. Charles felt blank. All he could see was Mike Burroughs' face, half gone, bloodied and lifeless. Mike was sitting in a chair talking to them about his brother whom he loved and missed so much and then he wasn't. He just wasn't as simple as that. Charles sat on the edge of the hospital bed with his feet dangling like a child. The bed was too high for him to touch the floor and there wasn't a little stool for him to rest his feet on. Shouldn't there be a little stool? There was always a little stool, a little step stool with shiny metal legs and a black rubber top. Every hospital room he'd been in at home in Toronto had one. Maybe it was a Canadian thing. A Canadian thing like being able to eat an orange and raisin tea biscuit without getting shot at through a picture window! There was a Canadian thing! Charles couldn't get over it. He saw Laurie's face in his head as she tried to help but a shot went off warning her to stay exactly where she was. That's exactly what it did. It warned her. Charles saw no evidence of that particular bullet coming in the window. It was a warning. The other two shots had been so precise- one in the eye and one in the chest. Someone wanted Mike Burroughs to die and they wanted him to die quickly. Who on the island would want the Burroughs brothers dead? The twins were tourists just like eighty thousand other people roaming the island at the moment. Charles would be surprised if they knew anyone on the island for more than a casual chat. They would know some of the JAWS fans but other than that, who? Charles' face gained some focus and his eyes narrowed. He was a bit more alert now than he had been. JAWS fans? Could it be a JAWS fan? Why? There was no evidence thus far that Mike or Sean had any bad feelings for any of the other attendees, nor that any of them had a distain for the Burroughs brothers. Charles thought that maybe he had better ask some questions. JAWSfest was over in less than forty-eight hours. If it was a JAWS fan, they

216

were running out of time to catch him...or her. Her. Well, it certainly wasn't Rebecca Thompson that was for sure. She was in a neighbouring examination room and under heavy sedation no doubt. If she didn't leave the island never to return, Charles would be completely surprised. What is it they say? No good deed goes unpunished? Rebecca had just been trying to see Mike back on his feet and maybe get some support for herself in the process. No harm in that. What did it get her? A smashed window, a bloodied chair, and a dead friend in her formerly pristine sitting room, that's what. It was sad. Charles was beginning to think that they would have made a good pair, Rebecca and Mike. Whether they had become friends or more than that, he could see where a strong bond of circumstance would have grown there. Well, it was all moot now. Jesus Christ.

Laurie walked in; she looked tired and older than her forty years. Her uniform looked dark like it was weighing her down rather than its usual stiff and bright. She looked her friend in the eye and put her hand on his shoulder, "How are you doing?" Her words were heavy with understanding.

"I'm okay. How are you?"

"I'm not going to lie; I've seen better days." Laurie managed a smile. "Has the doctor checked you out?"

"Yes. He said possibly mild shock. I think that's a catchall when he figures that he has to find something. Really, I'm fine." Charles smiled weakly back at the Chief.

"You look ok. I'm going back to my place for a stiff drink. Jeff is leading the crime scene investigation. He's a good man. I'm going to nominate him for Officer of the Year." Laurie walked toward the door. "I think that you should come with me. I've got twenty-four hours off. I don't think that you should be alone right now."

"You might be right. You have a spare room? I might need a good nap after that drink." Charles got down off of the bed.

"I do. I think that we both might." Laurie led the way out of the room and the two of them walked down the hall. Laurie pointed at a closed door. "Rebecca's in there. She's out cold. I don't know when she's going to be coherent. She took it pretty bad."

"I don't blame her a bit."

"Me either. I haven't seen anything like that since Boston. That kind of shit is why I left." Laurie shook her head.

The automatic sliding door slid open for them and they walked out into the bright afternoon sun. It took Charles by surprise that it was so bright out. It seemed like he had been in there for an eternity and that it should, by all rights, be night out by now.

"It's going to rain." Laurie said.

Charles looked up but could see no cloud in the sky. "It is? What makes you say that?"

"There's a nor'easter blowing in. You can smell it. I used to think the locals were nuts when they would say things like that but after you've been here a while, you pick up on these things. You mark my words; by tonight, you'll see a storm coming. I don't know what causes them but they're brutal."

"Nor'easters are generally caused by a shift in the upper atmosphere. The jet stream removes rising air faster than it can be replaced; that creates a storm. The northeast track drags it up along the coast and the counter-clockwise flow around the low-pressure system adds moist oceanic air. When this meets the cold air that's being forced south by the trough, the low pressure enhances the surrounding pressure gradient thereby increasing the existing spiral at a faster rate. The greater the temperature difference, the more turbulent and unstable the storm can become." Charles stopped talking when he caught Laurie's blank stare. "They can be a bitch."

She chuckled and shook her head. "Get in the god-damned car."

They drove the short trip from the Martha's Vineyard Hospital to the Chief's house on the point of East Chop. Laurie parked the cruiser in the drive closest to the front door and they got out. Charles scanned the sky for the nor'easter that the Chief had assured him was coming. So far- nothing. Once inside, Laurie unlaced her boots and pulled them off. She hung up her jacket on a wooden peg in the foyer and said, "I'll be right back. I need a shower. Do you want one? There's a guest bath."

"That would be better than great." Charles nodded.

"No kidding, right? Follow me." They both went upstairs and Laurie led him down the short hallway to a bedroom that overlooked the front yard. The bedroom was not big but it wasn't small either. It was decorated in yellow and white. Charles assumed that was to make it somewhat unisex but it was a little on the frilly side. Definitely a unisex room decorated by a woman. "You'll find everything you need in the bathroom. I'll meet you downstairs."

Charles walked into the bedroom and Laurie closed the door behind him. He heard it click. The walls were painted white and there were photographs hanging on the wall. All of the photographs were of various places on the island and each one had the colour yellow in it. There were photos of yellow flowers, yellow boats, yellow beaches, and they were all trimmed with white mats and dark wood frames. It was very effective. The room was quite warm from the mid-day sun beaming through white diaphanous curtains. Charles sat on the bed and began to take his clothes off. He lay back on the bed and promptly fell asleep.

*   *   *

"You're up." Laurie said as he walked into the kitchen. She was sitting in the sunroom watching the ocean and nursing a drink.

"How long was I out?" Charles rubbed his hands through his still wet hair. He had showered after his nap. He felt like a whole person again.

"About ninety minutes. I figured that you were sleeping when you didn't come down. I tried but I just lay there staring at the ceiling. That drives me crazy. So I got up. If I'm going to be awake, I'd rather be here than anywhere." She looked back at the ocean for a minute and then back at Charles. She lifted her glass and shook the ice. "Scotch?"

"Yes, I'd love one. I can get it. Where is it?"

"Cupboard above the fridge. Glasses are one to the right."

"Do you want a top up?"

"No thanks. I am already two ahead of you. I'll finish this and suck on some ice for a while." Laurie grinned but it was a solemn grin. "We have some figuring to do."

"Don't I know it." Charles got down the bottle of Chivas Regal from the cupboard over the fridge and a low-ball glass from the next one over. He poured in about two ounces and then got a handful of ice from the freezer and dropped it in. He took a sip and it burned slightly as it went down. He took another and went into the sunroom to sit on the couch beside Laurie.

"What do Karl Bass, Sean Burroughs, and Mike Burroughs have in common besides all being JAWS fans?" Laurie lifted her glass and slid an ice cube into her mouth.

"Well, that's just it. I've been thinking about that. Sean Burroughs was not a JAWS fan remember? He was here for Rebecca and Rebecca only. Mike was here for the festival."

"So they had nothing in common then." Laurie's tone was even. The scotch had calmed her down significantly. It was easy to see how so many police officers ended up with an alcohol problem.

"Maybe not but Karl Bass and Mike Burroughs were both JAWS fans and Sean Burroughs and Mike Burroughs were more than brothers- they were twins."

Laurie sat up straight and looked away from the ocean to look at Charles. "You don't think..."

"I had no reason to before but what if Sean was killed by accident? I imagine that it was dark in the hotel room because Sean was murdered in his sleep. They were twins. It's not that big of a leap. If that's the case, then it makes things a little simpler. There's a direct link between Mike and Karl and that link is JAWS. They were both on the island for JAWSfest; Mike was the biggest JAWS fan in the world; Karl Bass worked on the film and back at Universal Studios; Mike has even been to Universal Studios. It isn't much but it's a start. We finally have something to go on. It also explains why the murderer tried to cover it up with a shark attack. Who else but a JAWS fan would even think of that except maybe a fisherman but considering the cheap chum used to bait the animal, I think we can rule them out. Captain Hurtubise told us that. Pride is everything in that job. Well what do you think?"

"I think that Jeff is right. You should be a detective." Laurie got up and poured herself another drink. She thought for a few minutes before speaking. "You've been going to this festival a fair bit."

"Well, not as much as I had intended thanks to you."

"Fine but you've been attending and you've met these people." Laurie continued dismissing his remark.

"Yes. I suppose."

"Have there been any comments about Karl or Mike that you can think of that in hindsight seem a little odd or seemed odd at the time?"

"I don't think so. Everybody seems pretty even keeled. Well, there is one guy; his name is Tim Oakes. I don't really know anything about him except that I don't like him."

"Why not?" The Chief looked at Charles and he could tell that her brain was in overdrive.

"He's a liar to start with. He worked on the movie back in nineteen seventy-four. He worked in production. He was an islander but he made his way back to Los Angeles and kept working for Universal but- and here's something strange actually- I can't find any record of him after about nineteen seventy-seven. He worked at Universal all right but I don't think he worked there for very long although he didn't return to the Vineyard for a while. Karl Bass was an islander as well who went back to Los Angeles to work at Universal and there was a long history of his work on Internet Movie Data Base; Tim Oakes, there was nothing."

"So, Karl Bass and this Tim Oakes are both islanders and they both got hired by the same movie production company and they both left the island for Hollywood. That has to be our connection. There's no way around it."

"I think you're right."

"I think it's about time that I started talking to Mr Oakes and a few of the others." Laurie walked over to the couch and found her place beside Charles but when she sat down, she sat a little closer than she had been before she got up.

"Well, if you're going to do that you'd better do it soon."

"Why?"

"JAWSfest ends in less than two days. They'll be gone."

"We'd better get started then."

"We?" Charles finished his drink and got up to get another. He returned to the couch and sat down exactly where he had been. He wasn't sure how he felt about the growing affection between him and Laurie but the closeness was nice at a time like this; however, he didn't want to start something he couldn't finish. Laurie was a great girl and he liked having her in his

224

life. Messing up a romance could make her leave for good.

"You're not going to quit on me now are you?"

"I don't want to but I think that I am too close to these people to question them. At any rate, I don't want to end up being the Vineyard NARC." Charles laughed.

The Chief laughed with him. "Fair enough." She stopped laughing and looked out the window at the rolling ocean. "I think that you should stay here tonight." Her voice was low and a little shaky from nerves. Some things, you never out-grow.

"I'd like to but only if I stay in the spare room."

"You don't have to do that." Laurie looked him in the eye and spoke low. They were close enough that they could feel each other's breath. "I'm a big girl you know."

"I know that but you mean a great deal to me and these are not the circumstances in which we should be trying to forge a relationship. If it's meant to happen, it will. Don't you think?" Charles was scared that he had insulted her. "I find you very attractive Laurie but this isn't how I want it to go."

Laurie moved backward on the couch putting a couple of feet between them. "Saying all of the right things is only going to make it worse, you know." She blushed and smiled. "Some Police Chief, huh?"

"I think that you are a fantastic Police Chief and a fantastic woman. Let's just give it a bit of a wait, okay?"

"On one condition."

"Name it."

"We order an extra large pizza for supper, I get to pick the toppings, and we watch Young Frankenstein while we eat it!" She smiled and picked up her phone.

"Hey! What are you trying to pull here lady? Those are three individual conditions!" Charles mocked disgust.

"Nope it's all one condition but with sub-headings! I'm ordering the pizza now. Oh, and you're paying." She started dialling.

"Deal." Charles sipped from his glass again.

"Hi Vinnie, I need to order an extra-large with Italian sausage, tomato, green olives, hot peppers, onions, and anchovies and have it delivered to my place."

Charles' face lost its colour. "Anchovies?!"

22

"You missed all of yesterday! What happened to *having* to see Rodney Fox?" Jackie was right in Charles' face when he walked across the street to the Newes of America pub and ordered a pint of Stella Artois.

"Jackie, I would have much rather have been with you at *Swimming With Great Whites* than watching Mike Burroughs get shot in the face. You're just going to have to trust me on that one." Charles took a deep gulp of his beer and stared blankly at the bar. The beer was very cold and very good but it didn't do anything to erase the goings on of the last twenty-four hours.

"Oh shit! You were there? I didn't even think! Was it horrible? What am I saying? Of course, it was horrible. Oh, I'm so sorry Charles. Is there anything that I can do? What happened?" Jackie tried to rub his back but Charles shrank back from her touch.

You can just shut up and leave me alone, Charles thought but that's not what he said. "I'm alright really. I appreciate your concern Jackie but maybe I could just be left alone for a little while. Ok? I just need to regroup."

"Ok. You stay here at the bar and we'll all sit at the table. You join us when you're ready. I'll make sure you get some peace." Jackie walked back to the other side of the room and sat down with the others.

Charles was almost finished his beer when he ordered another one. He didn't like that he was drinking so much. Too often his family turned to alcohol to solve their problems and he tried to stay mindful of that predisposition. Just this once though, he thought. It's not like he was turning to the bottle because he couldn't pay his power bill on time; people had been murdered! Mike had been gunned down right in front of him. If that wasn't worthy of a beer or two or a scotch or two, he didn't know what was. His second pint arrived and it sat in front of him, waiting. The glass beaded with condensation as the cold liquid met with the warm room. Charles stared into the liquid amber and his mouth watered. Just like Pavlov's dog, he thought. That made him smile. Science always did. Charles wondered if drooling over a beer he had yet to taste fell under anthropology or just borderline alcoholism? Maybe alcoholism was anthropology; there was always a loophole- all in the name of science.

Last night, he and Laurie had consumed their fair share of Chivas Regal and they talked about the cast of characters involved in JAWSfest. How they proceeded from here on in was going to be very difficult. They had to talk to a few of them about Mike and Sean and about Tim Oakes. They would be talking to him as well but would leave him to the end. Charles was looking forward to that. Whether or not Oakes was guilty, Charles knew that he wouldn't care to be questioned. Oakes was the kind of man who took pleasure in seeing others squirm; it would be nice to get him in the hot seat for a change.

When Charles had woken up that morning in Laurie's guest bedroom, he had gone downstairs to a pot of freshly made coffee and Laurie cooking Vineyard farm eggs, Canadian bacon, and pumpernickel toast. It wasn't Edie's Edgartown Inn breakfast but it was delicious and had been exactly what he had needed. The hint of a hangover that had been threatening his frontal lobe was washed away by the salt, grease, and caffeine and he was good to go. Laurie had to go into the office and had no idea how long she was going to be. She was supposed to be off all day but Charles could tell that there was no way that was going to happen. She needed to be in there. She would take time off when she was dead. She couldn't take a day off in the middle of a murder investigation even though that's exactly what she would make one of her officers do- the perks of being the Chief. She had driven him into Edgartown and he had gotten out at the police station at 72 Pease's Point Way South. She would have driven him all the way to the inn but Charles had insisted that he get out there. He wanted to walk. He had toyed with the idea of walking from East Chop all the way to Edgartown but he decided that he just didn't have the time. Long distance walking was how Charles alleviated stress. It cleared his head. At any rate, the walk from the station had helped a little bit. The sky was greying over just as the Chief had predicted and the winds were picking up. Charles had wondered a couple of days ago what it would be like on the island when it rained. He was about to get his answer.

Charles drank his second beer at the bar in The Newes of America and he was almost finished when he felt someone come up beside him. It was Larry. "How's it going mate?" Larry looked respectful and grim. "Jackie told us what happened."

Charles nodded his head. "I figured. That girl couldn't keep her mouth shut if it was full of diamonds." He didn't laugh. "It's all right. It's not really a secret, I guess."

"Are you keeping all right? That's a pretty rough thing to go through."

"It was. It really was." Charles stared at Larry but saw nothing but Mike Burroughs.

"Why don't you join us mate? Help get your mind off it." Larry ordered a beer and another for Charles. The bartender brought them right away. "You're drinking Stella? Jesus Christ! No wonder you're depressed! What happened to your Guinness mate? That's a step down for sure."

"I love my Stella." Charles managed a smile. Larry was all right.

"Bloody Canadians."

"If I go over there and join the group, we'll all just sit there in dead silence trying not to talk about Mike's death. I'm going to sit here and finish my beer and then go for a walk on the harbour." Charles raised his glass to cheers his friend.

"Well, all right. I'm not entirely sure that I want you sitting at my table drinking that rubbish anyway. My offer was extended when I thought that you were still drinking Guinness. You come talk to me when you've got you're head sorted. Seriously though mate, if you need anything, Brooke and I are here for you twenty-four hours right?"

"Thanks." They shook hands and Larry walked back to the table.

By the time that Charles had finished his third pint he was feeling no pain. He made his way out of The Newes and waved at his friends as he went. They all waved and Larry made a signal with his hand indicating that Charles should call him. Charles nodded and walked out into the grey, windy day.

The Edgartown harbour was getting choppy; boats were clanging and banging in their slots. Charles turned right and walked along the shops and bike rentals until he got to the bottom of Main Street. He headed up Main to Water Street and debated heading south through Edgartown. He decided against it and continued up Main. He was going back to Starbucks in the Edgartown Meat and Fish Market. It was a good distance there and back and it gave him a destination. He would always end up at a Starbucks at home and a little homely familiarity would be quite comforting right about now. The wind was picking up and the flags that stuck out of every building were blowing proudly. Trees were all being pulled in every direction but leaves stayed put, holding on for dear life. Charles walked up past the Old Whaling Church and eventually past the Dairy Queen and on. Charles was trying to put the pieces together in his head. What did they know? They knew that Karl Bass and Tim Oakes both worked at Universal; Karl probably worked there for a lot longer than Oakes had. They were both islanders. Karl had come for JAWSfest but Oakes' reasons were still vague. 'Business reasons' is what he had said. The Chief would have to press him on that. There was no reason for him to tell Charles. Mike Burroughs had come for JAWSfest as well. His brother Sean had come for Rebecca. Charles figured that Sean's death was actually a case of mistaken identity. He had no proof of that but it made things a lot easier. If he wasn't then they had to find a connection that tied Mike, Sean, Oakes, Karl, and Rebecca all together. So far, there wasn't any such connection unless they counted Martha's Vineyard itself but if that was the case then everyone on the island was a suspect.

Charles walked into the Meat and Fish Market and inhaled the familiar deep, rich smell of his hometown coffee. It was as un-Vineyard as you could get but it was good nonetheless. He ordered his usual venti, non-fat, extra-hot Americano Misto. When it was ready, he sat down in one of the big brown leather chairs and relaxed. He was not ready to go back yet. He watched storm clouds get darker and swirl closer to the island. It hadn't started to rain yet but it was close. A smart man would go home now, thought Charles as he sat and drank his coffee. He didn't get up. He just sat and thought and watched.

About fifteen minutes later it started to rain and the Chief's cruiser pulled up in front of the market. Charles watched as she parked right in front of the door. Their eyes met and she shrugged and raised her hands as if to say, "What the hell are you doing?" When it was clear that Charles wasn't getting up, she turned of the engine and came in.

"What are you doing here?" Laurie sat down beside him in the next chair.

"Thinking." He said turning to look at his friend.

"Since when did you ever have to walk a mile to a coffee shop in the rain in order to do that?" The Chief took off her hat and relaxed a bit. "Say, these chairs are pretty nice. Is this the key to Starbucks' success because it sure isn't their fritters?"

"Yeah okay, you don't like their fritters. Give it a rest would you?" Charles knew that he was angrier than he should be but he didn't want her there.

"What's the matter with you?" Laurie was taken aback.

"I think that I've had enough. I think that three corpses was one too many for me. Especially since the third blew up in my bloody face." Charles suddenly realised what he had said. "I mean my face." He tried not to grin. "Not my bloody face."

"Nice one." Laurie smiled at Charles.

"We shouldn't be laughing! This is the most horrible thing that I've ever experienced."

"Yes, it is. Of that, I am sure; however, like Joni Mitchell said, 'Laughing and crying you know it's the same release'. If we don't laugh we'll end up running down the streets screaming! Don't be so hard on yourself." The Chief reached over and patted him on the knee.

"I'm so tired. This is exhausting. I was doing fine until Mike was shot and now I seem to be unravelling." Charles fiddled with his coffee lid.

"You're tired. That's understandable. You're probably not sleeping as much as you usually do and when you do, it's probably not restful sleep."

"No it isn't. Last night was rough."

"Me too." Laurie nodded.

"Really? That's good to know."

"Thanks a lot!" She kicked him playfully.

"I mean it's nice to know that it's not just me because I feel like I'm losing it."

"It's not you." Laurie smiled at Charles and they both looked out the window for a while.

Storm's a brewin' as they say, thought Charles. "Looks like you were right about the storm."

234

"Yep. We need to start taking a look at the JAWSfest people today. You don't have to come with me but if you could point me in the right direction, maybe give me a list of names and where they are staying, that would be a big help." Laurie pulled out a note pad and pen preparing to right down names.

"I'll give you a list but I'll come with you." Charles sat up straight in his chair.

"You don't have to do that. You really look beat." There was worry in Laurie's voice.

"I'm okay, really, just a momentary lapse. I'll be fine. Promise me no more corpses today. I'm done. I'll just make sure that I get a really good sleep tonight."

"Fair enough."

"Okay, let's start with Larry and Brooke Collins. They're good people. They'll be eager to help; they're honest and they can keep things to themselves." Charles said.

"All right." Laurie wrote their names on her pad. "Where do we find them?"

23

"What can you tell us about Karl Bass?" Laurie asked Larry and Brooke. Charles and Laurie each sat in wingback chairs while the other two sat on the couch in the Edgartown Inn library.

"Karl Bass from Facebook?" Brooke was the first to speak. Her expression told both the Chief and Charles that she was eager to help but not sure what was going on.

Laurie nodded.

"Not that much. I've never met him before. We chatted on-line but that's all. You met him though didn't you Larry? At the last JAWSfest?" She looked at her brother and then at the Chief. "This is my first one, you see?"

"You've met him before Larry?"

"Yes ma'am at the last JAWSfest like Brooke said but we weren't really tight or anything. I'm surprised that he isn't here on the island actually. He had said on all of the chat groups that he'd be coming for sure. If he's here, I haven't seen him." Larry sat quietly for a minute and then Charles could see a light go on in his eyes. "Do you think that Karl Bass is responsible for Sean and Mike's death? Is that why you're asking about Karl?"

Charles looked at the Chief and she looked at him and nodded. Charles answered Larry's question. "Karl Bass was the first murder victim. You read about him in the papers as a shark attack but he was dead before the shark got him." It took a couple of minutes for the shock of this news to sink in.

"So there have been three murder victims? Do you know that they were all killed by the same person?" Larry became much more animated than he had been when they had first sat down. Brooke sat quietly.

"They were all killed by the same calibre weapon." The chief said.

Charles looked over at the Chief. He hadn't heard that they knew that for sure about Mike Burroughs. He had assumed but there really hadn't been any proof the last he heard. The Chief nodded.

"I don't know what I can tell you. Karl seemed like a decent enough guy. He was a bit older than we were but that's all that really made him stand out. He was the same age as Oakes. That's who you should be talking to, Tim Oakes. They both worked on the production together and everything. They're even both islanders, I think. At least, Oakes is. Charles I told you that you should be talking to Oakes about this. Did you?"

The Chief looked at Charles. "Well, did you?"

Charles shook his head. "No, I didn't."

"Charles doesn't like Oakes that much, ma'am and I can understand that. He's a bit of a stuffed shirt. He likes to puff himself up on stories about working for Universal. Doesn't really ever talk about anything else much. It's kinda sad really to be walking around telling stories that happened almost forty years ago. I guess if that's all you've got..."

Brooke had pulled out her iPhone and was busy fingering the screen. She hadn't said anything but Charles watched her eyes widen and she handed the iPhone to her brother.

"Well, there you go ma'am." Larry passed it to the Chief. "That's Karl and Oakes."

The Chief looked at the phone and then up at Brooke. "Brooke can you email this to me please? Email it to Charles and he can forward it to me. That's a big help. Thank you very much." She passed the phone back to Brooke and she tapped at the screen a few times. It wasn't long before Charles' phone vibrated indicating the receipt of an email. He pulled it out of his shorts and opened the message. It was a picture of Brooke and Larry on South Beach at the last JAWSfest but in the background were Oakes and Karl. They each had an arm over the other and a beer in each hand. These were not casual acquaintances;

these were friends. Charles saved a copy of the picture to his phone (you couldn't be too careful) and then forwarded the email to the Chief. "I think that should just about do it." The Chief looked at Larry and Brooke. "You have both been a big help."

"That's it?" Larry looked surprised. No doubt he had been expecting a long gruelling sweat out under a bare bulb. He watched too many crime dramas.

"Unless you can think of anything else to tell me Larry, that's it." The Chief smiled. "I would like to ask you to keep our conversation to yourselves. I chose you first because Charles here spoke so highly of the both of you. He felt sure that I could count on your discretion."

Brooke and Larry nodded. "Absolutely."

"Do you need a lift anywhere?"

"No ma'am, I think that we'll probably just go back to The Newes across the street where you found us."

"I'll catch up with you as soon as I can guys." Charles smiled at his friends.

"Alright." The Chief stood up. "It's been a pleasure." The Chief shook their hands and Brooke and Larry left the inn. The Chief turned to Charles. "They seem very nice."

"They are. I like them very much."

"So? Who's next?"

"How about Tim McKenna and Andy Smith?"

"Where are we likely to find them?"

"Oak Bluffs for sure."

*　　*　　*

The Chief drove the cruiser up Beach Road toward Oak Bluffs and Charles watched the empty State Beach go by his passenger window. The waves were dark with white caps and the once inviting and soothing waters of the Atlantic were now threatening and mean. The winds rattled at the car as it sped over the bridge and Charles was slightly nervous. Laurie on the other hand seemed blindly unaware of their volatile surroundings. "Still thinking of moving here?" She said. Rain started pelting their windshield. She turned on the wipers.

Charles stared out at the ocean. "It changed so fast. It's still beautiful in it's own right. It's majestic and powerful." Charles smiled at the scene developing outside. "I really do love it here."

"You didn't this morning. Now who changes so fast?"

"Sorry about that. The island I love. I'm just not so keen on seeing my friends get butchered. Once we catch the man responsible, this will go back to being the paradise that it's supposed to be."

"So you are thinking of moving here?" Charles hadn't answered her question.

"I know that I'll be back and soon. That's a major decision though. I'm not in the right headspace to be making it either. I don't even know what I'd do to feed myself if I did."

240

"You'll think of something; you always do. I could really use a coffee."

There were no gulls outside the window. They had presumably all taken shelter from the storm. Most of the ocean that Charles could see now was white and frothy. The waves were at least ten feet high and the winds were strong. He was glad that he was in the car but he would have been even happier if he were indoors, curled up in his bed at The Edgartown Inn. It seemed that everything that he could see was a different shade of grey. The sky was almost black, a charcoal and the distant sea was a match. The water closer to shore was all a white grey froth that constantly slammed the shore. All of the trees blew almost sideways in an ashy and pale scrape. There existed no colour in this storm. He had never experienced a nor'easter in person and the whole experience was putting him even more on edge. At home, Charles enjoyed a storm but in a strange environment with no sleep and a murderer going after his friends, Charles would just as soon do without it. The car rumbled when the wind increased and even though he wasn't driving, Charles could feel it pull to the side toward the drop-off and the blowing brush and the sea. The Chief managed the vehicle masterfully and they stayed the wet and slippery road.

They came around Ocean View Park and drove down Circuit Avenue into downtown Oak Bluffs. The Lampost Bar was on the immediate left just past the Carousel. The Chief parked. "Stay here a sec. I'm going to grab the two slickers out of the trunk. No point in both of us getting drenched. I really should have done this in Edgartown." Laurie got out of the car and ran around back to the trunk. She got two bright yellow rain slickers out of the trunk, slammed it shut, and quickly got back inside the cruiser. When she got in, Charles saw little point in her putting on a raincoat. She was soaked. "Well that was almost pointless! Here put this on." She handed him a slicker and he struggled into it. "Alright. Let's go."

Coming in from such dark weather, the Lampost didn't seem as dark as it usually did. That same dark weather had kept a lot of the usual summer clientele home by the looks of things; it wasn't very busy. Moving toward the pool tables, Charles saw Andy and Tim McKenna right away. There were three games on the go. Tim and Andy were at the table closest to the back of the bar. The walls and the ceiling were white as were the exposed pipes that ran overhead. Each table was lit with a centre light of its own with a blue Bud Light shade suspended by a metal chain. Tim was in the middle of a shot but Andy saw them coming.

"Hey man!" Andy walked toward them and extended his hand. Charles shook it.

"Hey Andy. How's it going?" Charles asked.

"All right man but there's no chicks here. It's a freaking sausage party!" Andy laughed but he was serious.

"It's your shot dude." Tim walked over to them.

"In a minute man. I want to meet Charles' friend." Andy extended his hand. "Andy Smith, officer."

"It's good to meet you Andy. I'm Chief Laurie Knickles. I'd like to ask you and Mr McKenna a few questions if that's all right."

"Totally man! I mean ma'am...Chief?" It looked like Andy wasn't sure if he had just been insulting or not. Charles could tell that he was just happy to be talking to a woman.

"Chief will be fine." Laurie smiled.

Tim was less ingratiating. "What are these questions about?"

"What can you guys tell me about Karl Bass?" The Chief took a more serious tone when she asked the question.

"That he's M.I.A. for starters." Tim said. "Dude, totally bailed. Said that he was going to be here and that he had something big to tell me but I haven't heard from him for a week now. He hasn't answered any of my emails either. Kinda weird, if you want to know the truth. Why?" Tim set down his pool cue and picked up his beer.

"Mr Bass is dead. He was found a few days ago on State Beach."

"You're kidding me! That sucks dude! How did it happen?" Tim and Andy looked at each other in shock.

"He was murdered. Shot. The killer tried to make it look like a shark attack but it was murder all right." The Chief watched their reactions. Charles was surprised to hear her divulge that information. He had warned her that Tim McKenna was more than a little impressed by Oakes.

"Jesus. That's crazy." Andy said shaking his head. "So who do you think did it?"

"We're looking at some leads but right now we're just trying to figure out when he was last heard from or seen." The Chief looked at Tim McKenna for a minute before she spoke. "Have either of you seen Tim Oakes? I'd really like to talk to him. I understand that they have known each other for quite some time."

"Oakes wouldn't have had anything to do with this! Is that why you were riding him the other day Charles? Have you known about this all along and not told us? Dude I thought you were cool!" Tim shook his head and slammed his beer down. This was more emotive than Charles had ever seen him.

"Nobody has accused Mr Oakes of anything, Tim. We just want to ask him a few questions. That's all. As for Charles, any information that he has been privy to he cannot divulge while working with the police department; you must see that." The Chief spoke politely but sternly.

"I guess. I just don't like everyone giving Oakes a hard time. He's a good guy." Tim spoke almost begrudgingly.

"Do you know where I can find Mr Oakes?" The chief pressed him.

"No. I have no idea." Tim finished his beer in one gulp. "Andy can you order me another one? I'm gonna go take a leak...and take your shot dude." Tim slipped off to the can. The Chief looked at Charles.

"Thank you for your help Mr McKenna."

"I didn't help you man." Tim walked away.

"Sorry, Chief, he's pretty protective of his friends. I don't know where to find Oakes. We haven't seen him all that much. He said that he came to the island for business but he wouldn't tell any of us what that was. He picked up the waitress at Seasons the other night; he went back to her place, I think. Maybe she knows where he is." Andy smiled.

"That is very helpful. Thank you, Andy. Good luck with your game."

Charles and the Chief walked out of the bar and rushed back to the car. Charles got in but the Chief opened her door and yelled in over the weather, "I'm going to run over to Seasons. I'll be back in a minute." She closed the door and ran up the street. Charles sat in the cruiser listening to the patter of the rain hit the roof and windshield. He had always liked being in a car. The white noise of the engine had always made him fall asleep as a boy. Sitting in the car listening to the rain, as sleepy as he was, he was sure that he could drift off with very little effort. He had leant back on to the headrest when Laurie returned. He startled up right as she jumped into her seat. "The girl lives in Edgartown down past the school." She buckled her seatbelt and started the ignition. She turned the cruiser into Oak Bluffs and finally headed down

Barnes Road. Charles had never been down this road before.

"Where are we?" He looked around for something familiar but saw nothing. Actually, he could barely see anything period. The rain had become so heavy.

"You'll recognise it soon enough. I don't want to stay too close to the shore in the storm. We'll get more protection if we stay inland, I think." They drove straight until eventually turning left onto Edgartown West Tisbury Road.

"This looks familiar." Charles squinted out the window.

"It should. You've spent most of your vacation in here for Christ's sake." Laurie turned to smile briefly at Charles before turning back to the road. She didn't see the pick-up truck slam them hard on the driver's side but Charles did. The Chief was pinned to her seat by the door as it crushed inward. There was no other sound but the crushing screech of metal. They spun quickly across the water-covered road almost hydroplaning into the woods. The roof dented in. Charles was thrown into the Chief as they spun and the Chief's head hit the steering wheel with a sickening thud. The airbags inflated and Charles could see nothing. The wind was knocked out of him and he fought to breathe as the car slid further and further into the bush. His eyes bulged as he gasped. His stomach hurt. Finally the car stopped moving. It felt like it took forever but in reality it had been seconds. Charles gasped for air and his lungs burned as they tried desperately to refill. The Chief was out cold. There was blood at her temple. He could feel the blood coursing through his body as his heart pumped in overdrive. His hands and feet felt livid. They were throbbing. He lay very still for a moment while he processed what had just happened. Charles turned his head slowly. His neck was sore but he thought he was okay. He undid his seatbelt.

"I can see you fucking moving around in there!" A voice yelled outside in the rain. Charles recognised it. It was Oakes.

24

A single shot pierced through the windshield and into the seat beside Charles' head. This was not a car accident. This was an assault. Charles had never liked Oakes but he hadn't been convinced that he was capable of murder. That is until now. Charles tried to see what was going on outside the car but the storm made it impossible. The wind was loud; the rain was heavy; the skies were dark. He struggled out of the bright yellow slicker and left it draped over the back of his seat in the car. If he was going to try and make a break for it, he'd be better off in a dark wet T-shirt than a bright yellow raincoat. He opened the door as much as he needed to slip out and he fell to the thick grass below. He expected a shot to ring out immediately but there was nothing. Oakes must be having as difficult a time seeing as Charles was. When there was a shot, it was the yellow slicker that took the direct hit. It was much easier to see through the rain. Charles closed the door quietly and keeping low, broke away from the cruiser. He hoped that Laurie would be all right. There was nothing he could do for her right now except maybe draw Oakes away from the car. The bush was much thicker on the other side of the road. This would mean running out into open space, a much bigger risk. He knew that he couldn't stay where he was because he would be found sooner or later. Charles crawled along on his stomach through the thick mud and grass. He dug his fingers into the muck to pull himself along and they were starting to lose their feeling from the wet and the cold.

"You've been asking questions that you shouldn't be fucking asking, haven't you?" Oakes' voice bellowed out through the storm. He wasn't as far away as Charles would have liked but as long as he kept talking, Charles had an idea where he was. Charles didn't say a word. "I told you to stop riding me fucker! You and this bitch cop should have minded your own fucking business!" Oakes' deep, booming voice carried easily over the storm and it sounded like it was getting closer. Charles decided that he had to make his break. It might not be such a bad thing to have Oakes see him go into the woods. It would be easier to lose him in the pitch pine and scrub oak of Manuel F. Correllus forest. He stood up and looked back toward the car. Oakes' large frame was a black silhouette in the blowing rain of the storm. He was only about forty feet away. "You fucking idiot! Thanks for standing up! You're fucking dead now!" Charles turned toward the forest and ran across the road as fast as he could. He knew that as soon as he hit the forest he would be lost. Visibility would be nil and any noise he made would be difficult to follow in the wind. A shot rang out but Charles could tell that it wasn't very close. He hit the scrub oak at full speed and the branches jabbed and scraped his bare wet skin. A couple of the branches struck his face and came close to his eyes. He almost came to a full stop and began to feel his way with his hands. This was going to be a lot more difficult than he had imagined. Trees were down. Some were down from the storm and some had been down for a while. Charles stepped over some and crawled under the others. His clothes were slick to his skin and offered no barrier from the elements. He tried to make as little noise as possible. He figured that Oakes would have a difficult time hearing him but he wasn't taking anything for granted. Charles couldn't hear Oakes either; that wasn't good. He moved on in what he thought was the direction of the homes of Karl Bass and Rebecca Thompson. If he could reach a home, he could get a call to the police. Oakes may have taken out the chief but surely he would back off if he saw Charles getting help. Killing Charles in the woods would be Oakes' only chance. Charles' flip-flops were not making things very easy for him. They slipped off constantly. Charles' feet were cut and bleeding. Scraped and stabbed by branches and deadwood. He had tried taking them off but the ground cover was too coarse and it made stepping down impossible. He was shivering from the cold. It was becoming more and more difficult to concentrate. How long did you have to be exposed to the elements to get hypothermia? He was slipping constantly now. His hands were too wet and too cold to get a good grip on any trees for support. He fell into more trees than he was able to grab. He hit his head hard and fell to the ground. This was not how he remembered the Vineyard. This was not how he had expected to spend his vacation. He lay on the cold forest floor and felt the hard rain pelt on his skin. If he didn't get up, he would die here. There would be no more barbeques at Laurie's house, no more swims in the warm ocean, no more waking up in a warm bed at dawn on the Vineyard. He would die and Oakes would win. Charles could not let that happen. He sat up and then he stood up. It couldn't be far now. He shook his head and tried to focus. He started walking. It wasn't long before he came to a clearing. The rain was still coming down. It almost seemed heavier without the trees to block it but the ground was a lot more manageable. Charles took off his flip-flops and ran as fast as he could across the open space. The wet ground was muddy but soft on his bare feet. On the other side of the clearing he stopped. He was dizzy from exhaustion and it took a while for him to catch his breath. Charles looked back at the clearing he had just crossed; the rain was washing away his footprints nicely. Oakes could very well have gone in the opposite direction from the very beginning. He could be on the other side of the forest by now. On the other hand, he could be lining up a shot on the other side of the clearing. It was the not knowing that was the most terrifying. Charles wandered slowly under the new cover. It was nowhere near as dense as the last wood and it seemed almost manicured. Could he have found homes in the storm? Out of the rain emerged a large dark shape. He couldn't make it out. He got closer. It was a truck, a big trailer truck. Charles recognised it. He had found Karl Bass's house. This was the truck that Charles and Laurie had discovered when they came to the Bass home the other day. Charles checked the door; it was open. God bless islanders! He climbed in as fast as he could and shut the door.

The cab of the truck smelled of nothing but the pine scented air freshener that hung from the rear view mirror. Charles had always liked the smell because it reminded him of cars from his childhood. It seemed to Charles that they had been much more popular back in the seventies than they were now. At the moment, it was the sweetest smell that Charles had ever encountered. He sat in the driver's seat, panting from his trek. If Oakes was coming, Charles should be able to see him from his vantage point long before Oakes saw him. Charles found a blanket rolled up behind the passenger seat; he took off his wet shirt and wrapped up in it. Although he was still shivering and his teeth were chattering, it felt good to be out of the rain and wrapped in something dry and warm. He rocked back and forth and flexed and relaxed his muscles trying to generate some body heat. Charles figured that the truck might have saved his life. After he had warmed up and was a bit more stable on his feet, he would put his shirt back on and seek help in a nearby home.

At first, Charles wasn't sure that he had seen right but sure enough, there was a figure staggering slowly out of the storm. Charles could tell from the sheer size of him that it was Oakes. He looked a little shaky on his feet but he came nonetheless. Charles shrank down and made sure that both doors were locked. He peered up as high as he dared and saw Oakes coming straight for him. He got down on the floor of the cab and almost held his breath. Oakes tried the door handle on the driver's side and then a minute later tried the passenger side. Miraculously, thought Charles, he did not bother looking in the windows. Charles waited. There was no other sound but the rain hitting the cab. He heard the creak of the back door of the trailer open and then shut. Was the trailer not locked, he thought? If Oakes had the keys, it stood to reason that he would have opened at least one of the cab doors to look inside. Charles wanted to know what was in that trailer. If Oakes was looking inside and this trailer was parked at Karl Bass's house then whatever it was had to be significant in all of this. Charles knew that Oakes was behind this but he still didn't know why. He had to get a look inside that trailer. From his spot on the cab floor, Charles listened. He could hear the rain thumping on the cab roof. It sounded like pellets on the windshield. The heavy truck stood strong against the wind. It barely moved. He waited and waited but there was nothing but the storm in his ears. Charles got up from his spot of the floor and looked out the cab windows. Nothing. The only movement to be seen was the black and white violence of the storm framed by the cab windshield. The only thing missing was the Bernard Herrmann film score, thought Charles. He looked in the rear-view mirrors, still nothing. There was no sign of Oakes. Charles wondered if he had moved on. Had he gone into the Bass home to see if Charles had taken shelter from the storm? Had he gone in for shelter himself? Oakes was a big man but he hadn't looked too steady on his feet himself. Charles decided that it was worth getting out and taking a look. As much as he dreaded the thought of getting back out into the cold and the wet, he relished the idea of getting into that house. He needed to call for help. He might even risk a brief hot shower and change into dry clothes. There had to be something in that house. If Charles could change his clothes maybe even find a jacket, he might not even be recognised by Oakes at first. It would be enough to give him an advantage. Even the warmth would be an advantage. Charles got out of the blanket and put on his still wet and cold T-shirt. The slick cotton raised gooseflesh all over Charles' body but it had to be done. Cautiously, he opened the door. There was still no sign of Oakes. The rain hit him and stung his skin in remembrance of the freezing cold that he had experienced not that long ago. It would not be that bad this time around. He only had to get to the Bass house and it couldn't have been more than fifty yards away. Charles slipped down from the security of the cab and on to the soupy earth. He got down on his hands and knees and looked under the truck. There was no sign of anyone on the other side. Charles decided that he was indeed alone. Slowly he walked to the end of the trailer. He grabbed the heavy latch to the back double door and opened it. There wasn't much light so it took time for Charles' eyes to adjust. When they did. Charles jaw dropped open. It was a boat. It wasn't a whole boat but it was the remains of one that was for sure. The mast had been removed from its place in the centre of the boat and it lay on its side filling the length of the trailer. It seemed to be intact. The bow of the boat was intact. The window frames and the roof of the cabin were there, as was the steering platform on top of the cabin. The hull was gone and the transom was too. The name of the boat would have been on the transom but Charles didn't need to see the name; he knew this boat. This was the ORCA. So this is what it had been all about. These rotted remains of a forty-year old fishing boat. Mike Burroughs had said that the remains of this boat would get a half of a million dollars easy. Movie memorabilia was big business. Marilyn Monroe's iconic white dress had just sold for over five million dollars at auction. The camera that they filmed Star Wars on had sold for six hundred thousand dollars. Now, three people were dead over the rotted remains of Quint's boat from JAWS. They were dead over the boat that everyone thought had long been discarded by Universal Studios. Was this the business that Oakes had been talking about? He had worked for Universal. Was he the one who stole the boat or was it Karl Bass? Charles still had a lot of unanswered questions. Right now, he had to get into the house and make a phone call, he had to get Detective Jeff out to Edgartown West Tisbury Road to make sure that Laurie was all right. He hoped that someone had found her already. He was sure that she was just unconscious when he left her but the cold was brutal. The temperature had dropped so severely in the storm. There was also Oakes. There was no telling what Oakes might have done to her in his absence. Charles didn't think that he had given Oakes the chance to get to Laurie. They had started off into the bush pretty quickly but he couldn't be sure. Charles closed up the trailer and re-fastened the latch. He needed to get into the Bass house now. He was chattering again; his hands and feet were numb. He hurried in, what he estimated, would be the direction of the house. It wasn't long before he could see the outline in the storm. As he got closer, the dark silhouette started to take shape. Details became clearer. The Greek revival style home was dark from the wet but it was familiar and clear. This wasn't Karl Bass's home; it was Rebecca Thompson's.

Charles walked closer to the house. He was confused. Had Oakes come here to kill Rebecca? Had Rebecca even been released from the hospital yet? Charles wasn't sure. He walked up the steps to the side door and approached cautiously. Charles wasn't sure whether or not to try the door or ring the bell. He wasn't sure that he wanted to go in at all anymore but he needed that phone. There was no sign of forced entry. He reached for the handle. Before he could open it, the door flew open and Charles heart leapt into his throat.

"Well look who it is!" Oakes enormous figure filled the doorway and before Charles could move, Oakes swung his arm down and cracked Charles with the butt of his forty-calibre Glock. Everything went black as Charles collapsed onto the wet wood.

25

Charles woke up in a room that was probably a library or a home office; at least, that's what it looked like to him. The walls were lined with hard covered books and the furniture was covered in uncomfortable, hard, red leather. His head was throbbing. He lay still and did his best to understand what was going on. He knew that he was at Rebecca Thompson's house although there had been no sign of Rebecca. Charles wondered what Oakes had done with her and why. He tried to sit up and was almost nauseous from the pounding in his head. The pain rolled down from his temples to the pit of his stomach and back again, crashing against the inside of his skull like high tide. He lay motionless on the red leather couch for a few more minutes before trying to sit up again, a lot more slowly this time. Charles thought about Laurie. He hoped that she was all right. Was she still lying out there in the car with blood on her head in the middle of the storm? Charles couldn't bear to think about it. Someone must have come along and found her. Better yet, she must have regained consciousness by now. She was a tough girl. Sitting up, Charles could see out the window of the library. It was still raining but it looked to him like the storm had subsided somewhat. Maybe the worst of it was over. Charles had never been through one before; did they come in waves? He would just have to wait and see. The library door was closed tight but Charles could hear voices coming from the other parts of the house. He listened but they were barely audible. Charles could tell that they were arguing from the tone but they weren't clear enough to make out any words. He didn't like the idea of Oakes having a partner. Charles saw clearly for a moment through the pain in his head and the nausea in his stomach. The truth slapped him across the face. Oakes' partner was Rebecca Thompson. She had been stringing them along all this time. Oakes was the muscle and she was the brain. That had to be it. It answered so many questions, the more he thought about it. Oakes had come to Martha's Vineyard for a business transaction, he had said so himself. The business transaction had been involving the ORCA; it was sitting outside. Karl and Oakes had been employees at Universal; they must have been the ones to take the ORCA from the lot after it had been discarded and brought it here to sell it to Mike Burroughs. Who else would have been willing to buy it for that kind of money? His JAWS collection was legendary; that boat would have been the feather in his cap! Something had gone awry though; Karl had ended up dead. Oakes had shot him. Charles assumed that Oakes had decided not to share the money but if that was the case, how did Rebecca get in on the deal? There was no doubt that she was. Her paid bills were testament to that and the ORCA was now sitting in her driveway. Had she heard about the deal from Sean Burroughs at Nancy's last summer? Sean would have thought that spending that kind of money on JAWS was ridiculous. It may have come up. How long had this deal been in the making? Charles sat in the library staring out the window putting pieces together. Rebecca has lived on the island a long time; Oakes and Karl were islanders. If Rebecca was having money problems, and found out about the deal between Oakes, Karl, and Mike, she could have seen it as her way out of debt. She must have known Oakes from his island days. Sean was gone from the island but she keeps in touch, all the while seducing Oakes or was she rekindling an old flame? Oakes was the type to sit back and not question attention from an attractive woman. Rebecca could have talked Oakes into keeping the money all for himself. In fact, she could have held on to it for him. Did Oakes even know that she had spent a big chunk of it? Did he know that she was broke or was she playing the rich widow? If they killed Karl Bass, the only people who would be able to connect them would be the Burroughs brothers. They would have had to get rid of them too. Christ, why hadn't Charles seen it before? Rebecca was even the one to sit Mike in front of the picture window when he was shot! She had been the last one to see Sean alive. Charles had wondered at JAWSfest whether or not she knew Karl Bass. It had been staring them in the face. No such thing as coincidence. Those poor men. That was a lot of death for five hundred thousand dollars.

The library door flew open and Oakes' enormous hulk stepped into the room. He grinned a very broad and evil smile. He would have been a very good-looking man if his eyes weren't so black. They were filled with pure anger and hatred. "He's awake!" Oakes yelled to the unseen partner but Charles knew who it was already. Rebecca strode into the room with the same elegance that she had displayed on all of Charles' previous visits. She was wearing a white oxford shirt, very tailored jeans and the same string of pearls that she had always worn. She looked lovely. She certainly looked out of Oakes' league. It pained Charles to think of her in a partnership with this oaf.

"Hello Mr Williams. I am certainly sad to see you here." Rebecca looked at him as if to assess Charles' condition and possible threat to their schedule.

"I feel the same way Ms Thompson. I had thought better of you." Charles grimaced. There was no sense in grovelling for his life. They had already shot three people to ensure that there were no loose ends; he would be no different. Besides, Charles wouldn't give Oakes the satisfaction.

"You don't have a fucking clue what you're talking about asshole! She's a fucking genius. She and I have taken care of everything and we're off to Europe! So watch how you talk to her." Oakes face turned red as he barked in Charles' direction. He was her Doberman, anything to please his master. He took everything at face value. He just followed orders.

"I'm sorry Oakes but I think that I know exactly what's going on." There was no way that Rebecca Thompson would be hob-knobbing with her rich European friends with Oakes in tow. She'd be getting rid of him too once she no longer had a use for him. "How much money do you have left Rebecca?" Charles had to play his ace right now and he knew right away from the look on her face that he had played trump. Her veneer cracked just a little. "Oakes, did you know that Rebecca was broke and has used quite a bit of your ORCA money to cover her debts? She's spending your money Oakes."

"Shut up!" Rebecca's cool exterior was melting away to expose the fire beneath. "He'll say anything to get out of his situation, Oakes honey. Don't listen to him."

"That's not true is it, Becky?" Oakes looked at her with dog-like innocence. He tilted his head when he spoke to her.

"Of course not."

Charles pressed on. "Do you really think that she's going to take you around to all of her rich, classy friends Oakes?" Oakes looked at Charles intensely.

"She's going to get rid of you too, Tim. I don't know how but she will. You've done all of the dirty work up to this point haven't you? Has she done anything illegal? Has she done anything that would incriminate herself? You've done it all Oakes and for what? So she could spend your money. Ask her to show it to you, buddy. She should be able to do that shouldn't she?"

Oakes was not smiling and Charles could see that his small brain was having a hard time with all of this information. He was about to go off. Charles had to make sure that he went off in the right direction. "Where's the money, Oakes? She should be able to show it you right? It's your money."

"Shut up Charles!" Rebecca was a far cry from the cool, elegant woman who had entered the room. She had not counted on this.

"Where's the money, Rebecca?" Tim asked her directly.

"It's your money Oakes, not hers. It was your boat." Charles kept on but spoke very calmly. He couldn't risk having Oakes' rage directed at him. He needed to sound logical.

"Where's my money, Rebecca?" Oakes was focused on her completely now.

"I have it in a safe place, honey. Do not listen to him. He's messing with your head!"

"She should be able to show you your own money, Oakes. If she didn't spend it."

Oakes got out his gun. It was the same Glock .40 that he had used to knock out Charles. He was getting edgy. "Where's my money, Rebecca?"

"I have it! Put your gun away!"

"You're left handed Oakes aren't you? I saw that in the bar. Is that gun designed for a left-handed man? That would certainly make you look guilty instead of her. Did you get the gun or did she get it for you?"

Oakes stared at the gun for the first time in disgust. "She got the gun!"

"Why would she get you a gun that made you look guilty? Your gun points all fingers at you and she can't show you your own money! She's double crossing you my friend! You said it yourself, 'She's a genius.'"

Oakes was looking wild now. He was angry. Rebecca was frightened. She was backing into the room but there was nowhere to go. There was no way out. Oakes was between the door and them. Rebecca was inching toward Charles.

"Becky?" Oakes looked angry, scared, and wounded. He had put his trust in this woman and she had lied to him. It was clear to all of them now what was going to happen. Oakes' hands and face were livid. He was becoming purple and rigid. "You said we were going to Europe. You fucking cunt! You have been lying all along. Charles is right, isn't he?"

"No! No, he's not!" Rebecca started crying but Charles had seen those tears before. He didn't believe them any more than Oakes did.

"Don't give me that shit. You cried for Sean and Mike too. I'm not buying it Becky. I'll find my money without you! Good-bye Becky." Oakes lifted his gun and pointed it directly at her chest. Rebecca started screaming and this time- it was real. One shot cracked through the small room. Everything went quiet. Oakes stood in the middle of the room motionless and Rebecca fell to the ground, silent. Charles was frozen on the couch. Nothing happened for what seemed like an eternity and then Oakes fell face first onto the glass coffee table. It smashed completely. Charles winced in protection from the flying glass. Oakes was dead.

"Are you okay?" Chief Laurie Knickles was standing in the doorway of the library. She looked like hell but she was the most beautiful woman that Charles had ever seen. "Charles! Are you all right?" She repeated with some urgency.

"I'm fine." Charles tried to get up but sank back onto the uncomfortable, red leather couch.

"Are you sure about that? We'd better have someone take a look at you. That's quite the goose egg you've got there. Did Oakes give you that?" Laurie stepped over Oakes crunching broken glass as she went. She leaned over and felt him for a pulse. "Sometimes I wish I wasn't quite such a good shot...and then there's now." She stood again and walked over to Rebecca's limp body. "She's fainted. She'll be fine." Laurie stepped over to Charles. "He did quite a number on you. Detective Jeff and an ambulance are on their way. Shouldn't take too long.

The storm is breaking up." She sat down on the couch beside him. It was like sitting on tortoise shells. "Wow, this couch sucks."

"I know. I'll bet it cost a fortune too." Charles could hear police sirens in the distance.

26

Charles woke up in his bed in his guestroom at The Edgartown Inn. It was bright in his room and he could tell by the shadows that it was a lot later than he usually slept. He had been up pretty late. When the police and the ambulance had shown up at Rebecca's house, Rebecca Thompson had been handcuffed and escorted into the back of a cruiser and Charles had been put into the back of the Ambulance. Despite his arguments, he had been taken to the hospital for a thorough examination and a few hours of observation. After that, Laurie had come to collect him and take him home. She had wanted him to stay at her house but Charles had wanted to go back to the inn. He needed some time alone, some quiet. Laurie had assured him that he would get quiet at her house but somehow, even though the inn wasn't home, it wouldn't have been the same. He needed his own space. He was leaving today for Toronto and he just needed to regroup before he did. He had asked Laurie to meet him for lunch and then she could drive him to the ferry in Oak Bluffs. She said that she would be there for 11:00am so that they could spend a little time together on his last day. Charles sat up carefully, not sure exactly how badly his head was going to throb. It wasn't too bad. He had been given some Advil for his head and taken a couple before he left the hospital. They seem to have done the trick. He got out of bed and got dressed. He looked at his iPhone; it was 9:30. It was his last chance to have one of The Edgartown Inn's famous breakfasts- his last chance until the next time that is. He walked out into the body of the inn and Edie came rushing over to him as soon as she saw him.

"Oh honey, how are you doing this morning?" She took him by the arm and led him toward the garden. "The Chief called me at home last night and told me that you'd had a rough time of it. I think that she wanted me to keep an eye on you to tell you the truth." Edie winced as she looked at his forehead. "Oh, you did get the short end of the stick last night, didn't you?"

"I got the heavy end that's for sure. I'm okay Edie, really. One of your breakfasts sure sounds good though." He smiled at her. He was actually kind of enjoying the pampering.

"Absolutely. I'll get you a coffee. Same breakfast as usual?" Edie smiled her genuine smile at him.

Something was different about her today, thought Charles. "Yes, please. That would be great." Edie was wearing a pale pink blouse! The slacks were still black but the top was pink! She looked great. "Edie, you look beautiful in that colour."

"Aw, you silver-tongued devil! I sure am going to miss you when you leave!" Edie walked away with the appeal of a woman who knows that she looks good. It was nice to see.

The morning was sunny and fresh. All of the vegetation was standing at attention having soaked in all of the rain and was now straining for every drop of sunshine that could be found. The greens were more vivid and the colours of the flowers were more dynamic. The whole island was alive, desperate to put the tragedies of the past few days behind it.

Edie returned with his breakfast. Coffee, homemade coffee cake, two eggs over-easy, fresh baked bread perfectly toasted, and orange juice. "No charge for breakfast, hon." She patted his shoulder and went to tend to her other guests. Charles ate quietly. This was the first breakfast in a while that had not been marred with questions of death and violence. This breakfast was all about peace and quiet; it was about the stillness of a Vineyard morning in the mid-morning sun and salty air. This was why hundreds of thousands of people came to this little island every year. They had for one hundred years and probably would for another hundred. When he was finished eating, Charles sat looking out over the garden deep in thought. He had missed most of JAWSfest and his friends but they would find out why soon enough. They were probably reading about it right now in the morning paper. Charles didn't want to see it. When he was ready, he would look it up on-line back in Toronto from the comfort of his own living room in front of a fire. Finally, Charles got up from his table and made his way back to his room. He started to pack. He hadn't brought much. He went through the drawers and the bathroom and made sure that he had everything. He never set anything down where he was liable to forget it. Too many years of living alone had cured him of that. Being a bachelor made you very self-reliant. He was ready. There was just one thing left to do.

*   *   *

Charles walked up North Water Street for the last time before he headed back to Toronto. This would be his last chance for a swim before he left the island. That night he would be in his apartment and he wanted to be able to stand on his living room floor and look down to see Martha's Vineyard beach sand on his feet. Something about knowing that he had been in the ocean that morning while standing in Toronto always amazed Charles. He turned down the very familiar path across from the Harbor View Hotel and headed to the Edgartown Lighthouse and the Fuller Street Beach. The morning was perfectly still- odd for the island. No sign of a breeze. Was Mother Nature finally exhausted after the storm? Had she worn out her last breath? For whatever reason, the breeze was gone and the waters were almost still. The beach was deserted. Charles went to his usual area and dropped his T-shirt and towel in the sand. He kicked off his flip-flops and with a purposeful stride, entered the water. Once again it was the perfect temperature. The ocean was so receptive to his strokes that he seemed to move without effort. He glided away from the beach and the grass and the lighthouse into the warm, sunlight-speckled horizon. There were sailboats directly out from where he swam. It was impossible to tell just how far away they were; the water was so misleading. Distances looked shorter and further almost at the same time. The boats looked small. They looked far away. A luxury cruiser pushed its way out of the Edgartown Harbour and off into the open ocean. Everyone was going about their day like nothing had happened. Paradise was not lost. Charles continued to swim parallel to the shore away from the lighthouse. The salt water sweetly stung the little scars on his arms and legs from the nightmare of the previous day. It felt cleansing. The waters had also rid him of his headache. For a moment, the cool current sweeping over him had washed away everything that he felt he would have to try so hard to forget but never would. It was deep and black beneath his feet. The bottom was far out of reach. Charles watched as the sharp triangular sails flickered in the distance, sails of all colours- red sails, yellow sails, blue sails, and black sails. One black sail. One black sail moved differently from the others. It slowly got bigger, closer. One black sail. It was a dorsal fin.

Charles tread water in one spot. He knew that he could not make it to the beach. He was too far out. He tread water and almost didn't breathe. He tread water trying to move slowly and cause as little splashing as possible. He breathed through his mouth thinking that he would make less noise like he did when he was a kid playing hide-and-go-seek. The fin got bigger, closer. Charles didn't know how close or how far away it was but it was moving in his direction. It did not seem to be moving fast. He had never seen a shark in real life before. Did they move fast like in JAWS? It was closer now. Charles could feel his limbs going numb. There was no one to hear him scream and there was nothing they could do if they heard him. There was a Great White Shark headed his way. The black dorsal fin was about forty feet away. Charles could tell that the fin was bigger than his head. His heart was pounding. He couldn't help himself- he urinated. It was probably the worst thing that he could have done. The shark was there. Charles could see the wet blackness of his back and glimpses of the white of his belly. His mouth was slightly open allowing water to flow over his gills. Charles stopped breathing and did not know whether or not he was moving anymore. Charles felt his shin hit the hard pectoral fin of the enormous fish as it swam by him. It took forever to pass. It didn't seem to be circling him. It just swam by. The enormous sweeping crescent tail pushed Charles out of the way and Charles turned to see the dorsal fin glide off in the direction of the lighthouse. It didn't turn. It didn't go under. It just continued on its way. Charles tread water. He had never felt so much like an intruder. Slowly at first, he headed for the beach then faster and faster. He hit the beach and scrambled on to the shore unable to fathom what had just happened. What he had just seen. He would never experience that again. No one would even believe him. He couldn't say it out loud. Charles sat on the beach in his bathing suit staring at the ocean. His breathing was hard and heavy. They were out there. The most beautiful creatures. Charles sat on the beach.

*   *   *

The police cruiser pulled up in front of The Edgartown Inn at precisely 11:00am. Charles jumped in and they drove off down North Water Street. "Good morning!"

"How are you feeling today?" Laurie looked at Charles and smiled.

"I'm okay. I'm good. I went for a swim this morning."

"Are you sure that was a good idea?"

"It felt great." Charles smiled to himself.

"That's good." Laurie manoeuvred the car expertly through Edgartown turning onto Main Street. "Where do you want to have brunch?"

"I have no idea. Your call. I just have to be on the ferry at Oak Bluffs at one o'clock."

"My call? All right then." Laurie turned off of Beach Road and headed down Edgartown Vineyard Haven Road. In the late morning sun, the treed route was beautiful but given their last trip up Edgartown West Tisbury Road, Charles was mildly apprehensive. "How long do you think that you'll be gone?"

Charles had been wondering that himself. "I'm not sure. I've been thinking about that a lot. All dramatics aside, I love it here." He looked out the window at the trees and houses sailing past the window. Everything was quiet. This was how the Vineyard should be, he thought. "I need to spend more time here."

Laurie drove with two hands on the steering wheel and kept her eyes forward. "I'd like that."

"You are a big part of why I'd like to come back. Finding you here was unexpected and beautiful." Charles looked at Laurie but her eyes stayed forward.

"What does that mean?" Laurie asked.

Charles thought about his answer. He needed to know what it was as much as Laurie did. "It means that I will be spending more time on this island than I ever thought I would be. It means that hopefully one of my trips in the near future will be permanent."

"I'd like that too."

"Good." They drove past the Baseball Park and Martha's Vineyard Arena as they headed into Vineyard Haven.

"Figured out where we're going yet?" Laurie smiled and glanced in his direction.

"No. Should I?"

"Come on smarty. It's a Martha's Vineyard institution! You've got to go before you leave."

"Of course! The Black Dog Tavern!" Charles snapped his fingers.

"Black Dog Tavern." She turned the cruiser on to State Road and headed toward the harbour. "Well done."

Charles bowed in mock gratitude. "Thank you very much."

The Black Dog really was a Martha's Vineyard institution. It was founded in 1971 and it started as just a tavern in Vineyard Haven. They sold T-shirts with the eponymous dog logo. Charles remembered reading that in order to build up hype, they only let a certain number of people in their store at a time; line-ups queued around the block. The Black Dog now had several locations on the Vineyard and Nantucket and they had branched off onto the mainland as well. Charles remembered President Clinton had purchased Black Dog merchandise for Monica Lewinsky in the nineties. That would have been awesome publicity. Celebrities were always being photographed in Black Dog T-shirts. When it all came down to it, it was a great pub.

Laurie parked in front. The tavern was right on the harbour. The ocean lapped at its backyard beach. It was a beautiful spot. They walked up under the large wooden signpost with the dog statue standing guard on top. The tavern itself was the greyed shingle that was the island uniform. Laurie opened the white French doors and she and Charles stepped inside. Wooden floors reached out to wooden walls and wooden walls climbed to wooden ceilings. Historic black and white photographs hung on wooden posts and black and white signs from the whaling days of the island were nailed to every wall. The furniture was made up of classic wooden pub tables and chairs and most of them were occupied. As soon as they walked in, a waitress rushed over to them and greeted them cheerfully. They were taken to a table that looked out over the water and they sat down. They both ordered a coffee immediately. They didn't say much. They had thought that it would be nice to spend time together but there was an awkwardness about it. The inevitable emotional good-bye was hanging heavily over their heads. It was the proverbial elephant in the room.

"Not exactly the vacation that you had in mind was it?" Laurie grinned at Charles determined to make the most of the situation.

He laughed maybe a little too hard, forced. "Not even close. It sure was interesting though."

"I suppose that's true. The most interesting case I've had since I've come to the island- that's for sure!" She smiled. "You were a really big help. There's no telling whom Oakes would have hurt or where Rebecca would be by now without your help. Thanks Charles." Laurie looked at Charles with an openness that he wasn't prepared for.

"It was my pleasure. At the risk of sounding ghoulish, I loved every minute of it." He smiled warmly.

"Even running through the forest in a rain storm?" Laurie grinned at him.

"Well, almost every minute of it."

"So what are you going to do now?" Laurie asked him while looking at the menu. She had decided on ordering 'One Sweet World', two eggs, pancakes, and bacon.

"Well, funny you should ask that. I was thinking of writing it down." Charles had decided on the 'Shaggy Attack', two poached eggs with avocado, tomato, and cheese, on an English muffin with hollandaise sauce. He had always loved Scooby Doo.

"A book you mean?" Laurie had not expected that answer.

"Yes. Don't you think that it would make a good one?"

"I do as a matter of fact. I think that's an excellent idea. You're smart enough that you could pull it off. You're going to have to think of a good name for me."

"I was thinking of the name Penny. You know, kind of a play on Knickles. What do you think?"

"I like it." Laurie smiled.

"Good." Charles smiled right back. They ate silently for a while. He took it as a sign of good food, good company, or both. Charles remembered reading that the average silence between two people was four minutes long. After four minutes, most people started to get uncomfortable. Charles thought that it was a wonderful feeling to be with someone and enjoy each other without talking.

After lunch, they walked out into the sunshine. Before making their way to the car, Charles put his hands on Laurie and turned her to face him. She smiled up at him but then became more serious in anticipation. There was a way of looking at a person, looking right into them with no distractions. It was strong and intimate. It was a look of intention. Charles kissed her. He didn't kiss her hard but rather gently, softly. It was a kiss of love and exploration and nervousness but it was something they both wanted. She leaned into him warmly turning her face up into his. He took his time but stopped when it was right. He looked at her with that same intimate and important look. "I'm not sure where this can go. I live in Canada; you live here. I really enjoy being with you though and I'd like to spend more time together drinking wine, barbequing, laughing, and walking. Just being us."

Laurie's strong veneer was gone. There were small tears in the corners of her eyes. She cleared her throat. "I'd like that."

"But with less bloodshed." Charles smiled at her and they laughed.

"Yes. That would be good!" Laurie wiped her eyes. "I'd like that very much." Laurie was so beautiful when she let her guard down. "I need to get you to your ferry."

Charles boarded the ferry in Oak Bluffs, the same place he had stepped foot on to the island less than a week before. It seemed so long ago. So much had happened. There were more people on the boat this time around. Sundays were full of weekenders and vacationers. Wednesdays had fewer travellers. He looked down the long dock and saw Laurie in the distance leaning on her cruiser. She was wearing her full uniform and watching him go. He could still feel their kiss. It had been more than a kiss good-bye. It had been a romantic kiss and a perfect kiss. Information had been exchanged, phone numbers, addresses, email addresses, the works. Laurie did not have Facebook. In her position, she didn't think it wise. She was probably right. The horn blew and the boat started moving. Charles waved at his friend. It would not be long until he saw her again. Charles imagined that the island was beautiful at Christmas. If Laurie didn't come to Toronto for the holiday maybe he would surprise her here. It wasn't long before the boat was too far out for him to see her anymore. His gaze followed the shoreline as the boat lumbered past the island on its way to Woods Hole. They slowly wrapped their way around Vineyard Haven until eventually they were closer to the mainland than they were to the island. The sun was high in the sky and the clouds were few and far between. Sun gleamed brightly on the white deck of the ferry. Seagulls followed them out chasing the French fries that were being tossed in the air by adults and children alike. Some of them swooped pretty low. He looked ahead. Woods Hole was not far away. The trip wasn't long. Charles wondered how long the trip was exactly; he should have timed it. He would look that up later.

Fin.